Jessie Fothergill

The Wellfields

A Novel: Vol.III.

Jessie Fothergill

The Wellfields
A Novel: Vol.III.

ISBN/EAN: 9783337032197

Printed in Europe, USA, Canada, Australia, Japan

Cover: Foto ©Andreas Hilbeck / pixelio.de

More available books at **www.hansebooks.com**

THE WELLFIELDS.

A Novel.

BY

JESSIE FOTHERGILL,

AUTHOR OF 'THE FIRST VIOLIN' AND 'PROBATION.'

IN THREE VOLUMES.
VOL. III.

LONDON:

RICHARD BENTLEY AND SON,

Publishers in Ordinary to Her Majesty the Queen.

1880.

CONTENTS OF VOL. III.

—◆◆—

STAGE IV.

STAGE V.

THE WELLFIELDS.

STAGE IV.

CHAPTER I.

A REED SHAKEN IN THE WIND.

ELLFIELD'S position had not been altogether an enviable one, during the last few months. In his letter to Sara, summoning Avice home, he had casually mentioned having had money troubles, and this was true. He had shortly before heard from Mr. Netley, that now that his father's affairs were finally wound up, nothing would remain to him save three to four hundred pounds, then lying in the bank to his account, representing at most some twenty pounds a year. With this delightful information in his pocket he repaired one day to Burnham as usual, and during the morning had an interview with Mr. Bolton, in which that gentleman, all unconscious of what had happened, offered him the post of foreign correspondent to his house, at a salary of two hundred a year. He was surprised at the manner in which the proposition was received. Wellfield started, and exclaimed,

'Mr. Bolton—I—I cannot thank you—you do not know what this is to me.'

With which, leaning his elbows on the table, he covered his face with his hands. In truth, his emotion was almost overpowering ; this event appealed strongly to all the super-stitious elements of his nature. Here, when he had just been debating on his way to Burnham whether he should not that very morning explain his circumstances to Mr. Bolton, and then and there take his leave, leaving a message for Nita, and so cut the Gordian knot which he spent hours daily in futilely attempting to untie—now, at this very moment came the only man who could help him, and proffered him such tangible assistance that, it seemed to his nature, it would be madness to refuse it. A great strain had been put upon his nerves lately. He had expected and feared the news which he had that morning received, but he had waited for it as if paralysed. Now, everything, gratitude, necessity, convenience, pointed out to him that he must remain where he was. It was most improbable that anywhere else he would receive so much money, or be able to find work which he could do competently. Poor, weak and vacillating heart, which recognised honour and truth when it saw them, but which was too weak and vain to lay hold of them and keep them! Surely natures like his are more to be pitied than any others when their time comes for struggling and deciding—the natures which can see the right, but which *never* perform it, if the wrong offers an easier task at the moment.

Mr. Bolton was naturally surprised. 'Why, Wellfield,' he asked, 'what ails you ?'

Jerome lifted his face from his hands, pale and worn, and took the letter from his pocket.

'If you read that, you will understand what I must feel on receiving your offer,' he remarked.

'Ah, indeed! I *do* see,' said Mr. Bolton, when he had finished it. 'Yes—well, you need not fret so much about that now. Things don't look so bad. You have this salary coming in, and something to start with as well.'

'Yes—it is the feeling of relief, after all this strain which overcame me for the moment,' he answered ; and added, earnestly, ' Believe

me, Mr. Bolton, I shall never cease to be
grateful for the goodness I have received
from you and yours, all this time—I, of all
others !'

He spoke as he felt, and the remembrance
of Nita's goodness, and all that it implied—
of the miserable entanglement in the back
ground, out of which he could in no way
emerge with honour, let the affair terminate
as it might—all this brought a mist before his
eyes, and a lump into his throat.

'Pooh !' said Mr. Bolton, 'never talk of
that. We are not barbarians, to turn a
stranger from our doors.'

Jerome went back to Wellfield that afternoon, firmly resolved to write to Sara Ford,
and ask her to set him free. When it came
to the point, he 'could' not do it. He could
picture only too vividly what such a letter would
mean to her. It was Saturday afternoon. He
would wait until to-morrow, when he would
go up to Brentwood to the morning service,

and would see Somerville and consult with him. Perhaps he might even tell him the whole truth. He did not know. He went often to the services at Brentwood now. They soothed him, and he found a satisfaction in going there. Indeed, when one reflects upon the fact that there are many natures partaking of the characteristics of his, one sees how to these natures some form of religion, of an infallible institution outside themselves, and yet within their reach, is an absolute necessity ; and one begins to perceive more clearly why agnosticism has never been popular.

Wellfield could never have been an agnostic. He and such as he have not the mental and moral toughness of fibre which enables a man to contemplate the mystery of the heavens above and the earth beneath ; of the life and the death, and the pain and the evil that are upon the earth, of his own feelings and speculations, and their origin, and the purpose and destiny of them—and then, while reverently owning 'I know nothing, and I will assert nothing, upon these things,' has yet the courage to live up to an ethical code as high, as pure, and as stern as that of St. John or of Christ—expecting nothing from a life to come, as to the existence of which he is in absolute ignorance. The more part of mankind want none of this; they want a religion, a thing that will let them sin, and prescribe to them how they must get forgiven. · Such a religion was found in perfection at Brentwood, and thither Jerome repaired.

There was an unusually splendid service that morning. A great dignitary—a cardinal —preached. The sermon set forth eloquently the rewards of faith and obedience. He assumed that all present had overcome the initiatory difficulties, that they were all entirely faithful and entirely obedient; and then he proceeded to depict their happiness even here upon earth, not to mention the joys which awaited them in heaven.

Wellfield listened ; he saw others listening : a haughty-looking woman in widow's weeds, just on the other side of the aisle. She was Mrs. Latheby of Latheby, whose only son was being educated at Brentwood. He knew her well by sight ; her pride and reserve were proverbial. Yet she wiped tears from her eyes as she listened to the sermon. There was a profound silence—a silence full of suppressed emotion, as the sermon progressed. Faith and obedience ; nothing to do but submit that private judgment which is usually so ill-trained, and which invariably causes such trouble, and *ye shall have rest unto your souls.*

That was the burden of the discourse—that was what echoed with so seductive a sound in Wellfield's ears.

After the service he saw Somerville ; he was presented to Mrs. Latheby, who remem-

bered his mother, and told him so; adding
with the regretful smile which lent such pathos
and sweetness to her proud and still beautiful
face :

‘ Ah, Mr. Wellfield, if that beautiful mother
of yours had been here to-day, how happy
she would have been in what she had heard
. . . and it gives me a melancholy pleasure to think that had she lived to bring
you up, you might have been standing
here, one of us, not a looker-on, out in the
cold.’

‘ You are far too good, madam, to think of
me at all,’ he replied, moved somewhat by
her words, and yet under the influence of the
emotion which the cardinal’s word-picture had
aroused.

‘ I must ever take an interest in the only
son of Annunciata Wellfield,’ she answered ;
‘ and I want you to come and see me—will
you ?’

‘ I shall only be too honoured.’

'Then I shall write this week, and appoint a day for you and Mr. Somerville to dine at Latheby—if you can come, father.'

'I shall no doubt be able to come,' replied Somerville.

Mrs. Latheby waited in the parlour to have an interview with his Eminence. Somerville walked with Wellfield along the lane towards his home. Wellfield told him what had happened.

'I am superstitious, I suppose, acccording to your notions,' said Somerville, 'and I call it a sign.'

'I do not call it superstition,' stammered Wellfield. 'I have myself been thinking to-day that—that——'

'That you ought to follow my advice, and ask for Miss Bolton's hand,' was the firm, decided reply.

'If it were not for this miserable business in the back-ground——'

'It is your duty to tell the truth to one

lady, or to get some one to do it for you,' said Somerville, in a smooth, even voice, which yet cut his hearer like a whip. He winced.

'If you mean to stay here, you ought at least in duty and honour either to propose to Miss Bolton, or to tell her that you are bound to another woman.'

'Do you suppose I don't know that ?' retorted Wellfield, almost fiercely. 'Have I not been debating within myself until I am almost mad, how to tell her.'

'You are nervous, perhaps. Would you like me to do it for you ?'

'You — heaven forbid !' he exclaimed passionately. 'That would be to ruin—I mean, I must think about it again. I will dicide to-morrow.'

'As you are taking the matter into con- sideration,' observed Somerville, with scarcely disguised insolence, 'I would really strongly advise you to reflect whether it would not be in every way more advisable to tell the other lady that you wish to be free.'

' Do you wish to insult me ?' asked Wellfield, pale with passion.

' To insult you! I am simply trying to advise you for the best. Remember, you are now dependent upon this post of Mr. Bolton's. If you, or anyone else, lets Miss Bolton know that you are engaged elsewhere, it might be bad for your prospects. Girls who have an idea—however mistaken—that their feelings have been trifled with, are apt to be vindictive.'

There was a palpable sneer beneath the even politeness of his tone. He had taken out the whip—the whip which Wellfield's own pleasant sins had knotted into a cord, and which his own weakness and vacillation had put into the other's hand. The very first stroke had drawn blood. With a chest heaving convulsively, and a glitter in his eyes of anything but agreeable import, Wellfield clenched his hands behind him, and said, composing himself with an effort rendered efficacious by dire necessity.

'I see what you mean, but I must think about it.'

'Yes, do,' retorted his monitor, with a smile. 'And I must return, or I shall receive a reprimand. Good-morning. I will stroll down to Monk's Gate to-morrow evening. Shall I find you in ?'

'I expect so,' said Wellfield, sullenly.

They parted. Somerville smiled as he took his way towards Brentwood.

'He will come back,' he thought. 'He has gone too far. He cannot do without me . . . and he is half won. Mrs. Latheby must flatter him, as she *can* flatter for us and for her Church. He will come. I see him coming. And when he is married to Miss Bolton, of course she must learn the truth, or they might live in such harmony that my game would be spoiled.'

Somerville called early on the following evening, and it was during this visit that the arrangements were made for Avice's return. Jerome was thankful for the suggestion. He dared not go to fetch her himself. He dared not face Sara. But one side of his character —his pride, we must call it, for want of a better name—the pride which did not prevent him from making love to one woman while solemnly engaged to another, pricked him sorely at the idea that Avice was receiving Sara's kindness and living under her care. He did not know how he was to explain it, nor did he much care. He was getting callous, and reckless, and anxious only to find a way out of the coil. Somerville had received his orders suddenly, and was to set out almost immediately. Perhaps the visit of his Eminence had something to do with the matter. He had had a long conversation with Father Somerville, and had bestowed his blessing

upon him before parting. Jerome according-
ingly wrote that letter to Sara, and on the
following morning Somerville set out on his
travels.

CHAPTER II.

A CONSUMMATION.

NE afternoon, on returning from Burnham, Jerome found a letter awaiting him. It was that which Somerville had written from Elberthal, and it set Wellfield's heart on fire. Somerville in his calculations had not forgotten to reckon among the possible effects of his communication that one which might lead Jerome to rush back again to Sara's feet, shocked into honesty by the fear of losing her. But the priest had decided again, 'No; he will remember that if he leaves Mr. Bolton he leaves all his subsistence; that his sister is

on her way home, and he has nowhere to
place her; and above all, that he cannot
present himself to Miss Ford in the character
of injured innocence, considering the manner
in which he has been conducting himself.
Besides, it will be so much easier for him to
stay where he is and propose to Miss
Bolton.'

Whether by chance, or in consequence of
extreme and almost superhuman cleverness,
Somerville had managed to calculate with
mathematical correctness. Wellfield's first
impulse, on reading the letter, was to rush
off then and there in all haste, and never to
pause until he had found Sara, and clasped
her in his arms, looked into her eyes, received
the assurance of her love. Then, across this
fever of impatience came the thought,
creeping chilly :

' When she turns and asks you to explain
your late treatment of her, what are you to
say ?'

He knew she might love with an utter abandonment of self; but should she once suspect falsehood, it would all have to be disproved, all made clear and clean, before she would touch his hand and speak tenderly again. And it was too hard, too cruel. Avice was on her way home. Sooner or later Sara would learn something of what had transpired here, at Wellfield . . . What was all this talk about her favouring some other man ? Again the impulse was strong, if not to go to her, to seize pen and paper, and ask what it all meant. And again came the cruel, sudden check. She would have a perfect right to retort with a similar question —to ask him what his conduct meant—to demand a reason for his late ambiguous treatment of her. He might not write. He buried his face in his hands and groaned. What was he to do ? His counsellor was away. For the first time he realised, by the intensity of his wish to see him, what a hold Somerville had gained upon his mind.

It .was a dreary, gusty November evening. Round the solid walls of the old house of Monk's Gate, the wind wuthered sadly and fitfully; the deep-set lattices did not shake— one only heard the sound of the wind. No passing vehicles disturbed the ear. The quiet country road was profoundly still.

No one came to relieve his solitude, or to divert his mind from its miserable debate with his conscience. He sat there perfectly alone, until at last he could bear it no longer. He would go to the Abbey, and join them there. There would be cheerful voices, honest faces; words to listen to—not this hideous silence, broken only by the dismal sighing of the wind about the roofs, and in the trees.

He snatched up his hat, opened the door, and sallied forth into the night. The Abbey gate was close at hand. Soon he was within that dark portal, beneath the now leafless

avenue which shaded the river walk ; he could
hear the swollen stream rushing noisily along.
He saw a light in the drawing-room windows,
and, with an effort, he gathered himself together, so as to appear composed and collected,
for they would not understand his disturbance,
and the fear lest by betraying it he should
'appear unto men a fool' was sufficient to
give him outward calm.

Of course, when the servant opened the
door, Wellfield asked for Miss Bolton, and
was told she was in. But he was in the habit
now of going unannounced into the drawing-
room. The page knew it, and retired.
Jerome hung up his hat, took his way to
the drawing-room door, and with a brief pre-
liminary knock, entered.

A large fire was burning in the ample grate,
but no lamps were lighted. No one was in
the room, either, except Nita, who was kneeling upon a tiger-skin, straight in front of the
fire—her dog Speedwell by her side. Her

hands were clasped before her; her eyes wide open, and her cheeks, with them, exposed to the full fierceness of the glowing fire.

But she heard him come : heard his footstep, and started up—a deeper blush mantling through the red which the heat of the fire had called forth.

Jerome came slowly up to her, and stooped over her, and the firelight shone into his eyes, and showed the hollows in his pale cheek.

'Are you quite alone?' he asked, and there was no surprise in his accent, for it had flashed upon his mind, as he came in and found her by herself, that perhaps this too was a 'sign,' as Somerville had called it.

'Yes,' replied Nita, rising to her feet. 'Papa has gone up to Abbot's Knoll, to see John : it is a wonder for him to be out, as you know. I don't know what plots they are concocting, I'm sure. John is perfectly mad about some bird—a reed-warbler, he calls it—

which he vows he has found by the river here, and he is going to overthrow some great authority, who says they are never found so far north.'

'And Miss Shuttleworth ?' asked Wellfield, unconsciously acting on his secret desire to know the coast clear.

'Aunt Margaret has got a tea-party of school-teachers. She always has one about this time. . . . Did you want to see papa ?'

'I am afraid I don't quite know what I want,' he answered, with a great sigh of exceeding weariness, as he rested his elbow on the mantelpiece, and looked at her with his sombre, mournful eyes. 'I don't think I do want to see your father—at least, I felt very glad when I saw you alone. I think I want to escape from myself and my thoughts, Nita.'

'Why, do your thoughts trouble you ?' she asked, softly and timidly.

'Sometimes they do, very much—to-night particularly. Will you let me sit with you a little while, or must I go back again to Monk's Gate and solitude ?'

' Oh, Mr. Wellfield, you know that you are always welcome here, when it pleases you to come !'

' That is a good hearing,' he answered, and such was the odd mixture of the man's nature, he felt that it was good. He felt that from Nita he would receive no blows or buffets, or rough words—nothing but (metaphorically speaking) tenderest caresses and softest whispers. To go back to solitude, and the harsh accusations of conscience, and the disagreeable anticipations for the future, was not in him ; so he stayed.

' Do you never feel restless ?' he went on. ' Do you never feel as if you would like to set off on some indefinite journey, and without knowing where you were going—with a sort of " onwards—but whither ?" feeling,

that you would just like to go on and on, and
for ever on, till life itself came to a stop?
Have you never felt it?'

'Yes, often,' said Nita, in a low voice.
She was standing opposite to him, on the
other side of the fireplace. Her hands—
soft, pretty, little white hands—were folded
lightly one over the other. Jerome, in his
idle sentimentalising, had time to notice that
she had on very pretty black-lace mittens,
and that the stones of some rings sparkled
through them; that a gold bracelet was pushed
tightly up the rounded arm. He scarcely observed her averted face—her eyes looking
into the fire; her rapidly-heaving bosom; and
he prosed on, because he liked talking to her
—because it was easy to make himself out
sad, and blighted and persecuted.

'I felt sure you had,' he said. 'That is
what I feel to-night. But for your father's
goodness to me—but for the stern mandate
of reason and necessity and common sense, I

would set off now, this moment ; and leave Wellfield, never to return to it.'

He had spoken this time without rhyme or reason ; without any *arrière pensée*—any calculation as to the effect his words might have upon her ; and when he saw what it was, even he was startled.

' Leave Wellfield! Go away !' she exclaimed, turning suddenly pallid. ' What makes you say such a thing ?'

' Should you care much if I did ?' he asked recklessly and ruthlessly. ' Would it —can I believe it would make any difference to you ?'

He was standing before her, looking, as the girl in her sad infatuation thought, so noble, so calm, so undaunted, after all his misfortunes—undisturbed—only sad and a little despondent after his reverses—more of a hero than ever. Ah ! if she might only tell him what she felt and wished ! But at the moment something held her back ; she

could not say all—could not speak the words
her heart was breaking to utter. She drew
a long breath, and said :

'You—it would make me very sad if you
went away, for then I should feel more than
ever what interlopers we must seem to you.
I should feel that we had driven you out
from your old home. And you speak of
papa's goodness—but *is* it goodness? I
don't call it the work for you—drudging in
an office in that way, like some common
clerk. I should think after a time it would
drive you almost mad.'

'Oh no! It is only the getting into
harness that is such hard work—the learning
how to become a machine. I fancy when
that is accomplished, and the routine mastered,
one can go on easily enough—almost unconsciously. I shall get used to it sometime.
Meanwhile, I am thankful to be so well off.'

'You are not thankful to be well off when
you know you are very ill off,' said Nita,

with agitation. 'And you will never get
used to it. If you could you would not be
what you are—it would not all be so horrible.
. . . Oh, I wish the Abbey—I wish the money
were mine, that I might ask you to take
it as your *right*—your inheritance! But
I can do nothing, nothing; I am power-
less, helpless, and I believe it will kill
me!'

She turned away and threw herself upon a
couch, burying her face in the cushions, and
trying to stifle her sobs. For, with a great,
overwhelming rush, the conviction had come
to her of what she had really said—a sense
of intolerable shame, an agony of humiliation
was torturing her.

For one moment Wellfield gazed at her,
at the prostrate form and heaving shoulders,
convulsed with sobs. Then he made a step
to the sofa, and knelt down beside her.

'Nita!' he whispered, 'dear Nita! Look
up! I want to speak to you.'

But she would not raise her face, exclaiming in a broken, stifled voice :

' No, no ! don't ask me ! I cannot look at you. I can never look at you again. Oh, leave me ! Mr. Wellfield—Jerome ! for the love of heaven leave me, or I shall die—I shall *die* of shame !'

' You shall not die of shame,' he said, in the same low, persuasive voice. ' Nita, you shall look at me, my good angel, and hear what I have to say to you.'

With gentle but irresistible force he drew her hands away, and lifted her head, and made her look at him, and in that moment he had, perhaps, forgotten the existence of Sara Ford.

' Why do you speak of shame, Nita ?' he asked, looking tenderly into her piteous face. ' What shame can there possibly be in giving way to such a generous impulse, and in showing a lonely, fallen man that there is one sweet woman left who cares for him, and would make him happy if she might? Heaven bless you, dear, for such goodness. But you know—you must know, why I cannot take you in my arms and say, "I accept that goodness, and offer you my life's devotion in return for it." You know it would be the basest conduct on my part towards your father, who has treated me with unheard-of goodness. I know he wishes you to marry, and I know he would consider it the height of presumption in *me* to ask for you.'

'Oh, don't speak of such things—of marriage and such horrors!' she almost moaned, struggling to free her hands; but he went on:

'No, I must face my future as best I may, and it will be with the better cheer from the knowledge that goodness such as yours exists —goodness which I worship and honour all the more in that you have made it known to me.'

'Oh, don't! don't speak of it! I cannot bear it!' she cried, wrenching her hands away, and again covering her face from his sight. She felt as if she were in some strange, delirious dream. Wellfield's looks and tones thrilled through every nerve. Did he love her? Did he mean that if he dared, he would tell her so? She knew not what to think. She only knew that *he knew*, and that say or do what she might, she could never undo the fact that she had betrayed herself; and that the one thing which would have made it all right —would have made the difference between a nightmare and a vision of Paradise—the knowledge that he loved her—was wanting. Yes, despite his caressing tones, his eloquent eyes, his tender words, she did not understand that he loved her.

'Do not be so distressed,' he said. 'I will never speak of it again, if you desire me to be silent. I will forget it—anything—only, dear, do not be so unhappy!'

' I hear them coming,' said Nita, her ear
preternaturally quick. ' I hear their voices.
I cannot see them—they must not see me.
Tell them—tell them I am ill—for I am—
and—let me go !'

' Yes—stop one moment, Nita !' he answered, clasping his arm round her waist, as
she was darting past him.

' Let me go !' she breathed again, but her
voice died away as his lips met hers—once and
again, and he said, in a low, passionate voice :

' There ! We have that, whatever may
happen in the future. Nita—*my* Nita !'

He loosed his arm, and she had flashed
past him, and out of the room, in a second.

Jerome was left standing on the rug, feeling, he too, as if he had just gone through
some mad fit of delirium. What had hurried
him on to that act of a moment ago ? He
stood with bated breath, and eyebrows drawn
together—then breathing again, a long, nervous breath, he muttered :

' By G—, I am a villain !'

And in the moment that ensued between
this confession of conscience, and the entrance
of the others, he had time too to realise that
one cannot be a villain one moment, and have
done with the villainy and its effects in the
next instant.   One woman's heart, at least,
must go near to break, in punishment for
his sin of this night—or rather, for this night's
consumnation of his sin.   It lay with him to
decide which woman must suffer—Nita, who
was here, close by, and whose agonies he
must watch ; or Sara Ford, away in Elberthal, and alone, now—and whom he would
not be able to see, let her have what she
might to endure—Sara, who had loved him
all along—who loved him still, as he knew,
and would have known, had fifty letters come
to tell him how devoted she and Rudolf Falkenberg were, the one to the other.   Which
woman was to have the blow from his
cowardly hand ?

An ugly problem ; one which would require answering very soon—but not to-night. It might be delayed till to-morrow.

He felt a sense of relief at this, as Mr. Bolton and John Leyburn came in, and they began to ask him why he was alone, and what had become of Nita.

The three men supped alone that night. When John Leyburn was departing, and Wellfield was about to go with him, Mr. Bolton stopped him, saying he wanted to speak to him. Jerome, still thankful to have excuses which delayed his home-going, re- mained willingly. One other surprise was in store for him that night. Mr. Bolton, in his usual stilted and pedantic, but most distinct and unequivocal style, informed him that he had that evening been taking counsel with John Leyburn, as his most trusted friend, upon several important matters. That in the main John agreed with him, and that he wished to lose no time in telling him, Jerome Wellfield, that, after profound consideration, he had come to the conclusion that it would be for his own pleasure and his daughter's happiness if a marriage between her and him—Wellfield—could be concluded.

'If you feel warranted, by your feelings towards her, in proposing to her, you have my permission to do so. If not—you will excuse my speaking plainly—your visits here will have to cease, for I do not wish her happiness to be imperilled.'

Wellfield passed his hand over his eyes : he was almost stunned. At that moment things stood out clearly, and, so it seemed to him, the right bearings of them. To think of ever marrying Sara now was hopeless. Love must be cast aside, and duty embraced instead. He was perhaps not conscious that he was elaborately and ingeniously evading and concealing the truth, when he said :

'But for feeling sure that I should displease you exceedingly, and that it would be an ill return for your benefits, for a penniless fellow like myself to speak to her, I should have proposed to her to-night.'

Mr. Bolton's face brightened.

'Ah !' he said, ' I knew there was a liking on both sides. That makes it smooth. Propose to her to-morrow morning, instead of to-night. `You will have her to yourself, for I shall be in town.'

They shook hands, but Wellfield's eyes did not meet those of Mr. Bolton as he went through the ceremony. He went away. Then it was upon that proud head of Sara Ford that the stroke was to fall, and he was the miserable wretch whose hand was to deal it.

CHAPTER III.

WELLFIELD, at last left alone to ponder upon his position, felt himself in thoroughly evil case. Once or twice a wonder crossed his mind as to whether there were yet time to turn back, retrace his steps along this dire and darksome path; fight his way back to the light, and to Sara Ford; confess everything, and put himself and his fate in her hands. He had a longing to do it, but when he reflected what that course involved, he had not the courage. It was to lose every assured present advantage for a problematical one; for he could not—at least he said so to himself—be sure that Sara would forgive; and if she did not——

He followed Mr. Bolton's advice, and it struck him once or twice that it was an unusual thing for a man in Mr. Bolton's position to have deliberately invited a ruined man like himself, without friends and without references, to marry his only daughter, and enter his family. Perhaps, had he heard Mr. Bolton's confidential conversation of the night before with John Leyburn, he might have felt the distinction less flattering. John and Mr. Bolton had agreed that a great change had come over Nita, and both of them, though they did not openly speak it out, and confess it, owned tacitly that they considered that change had been brought about by her feelings for Jerome Wellfield. And Mr. Bolton had said :

' He'll never be any great shakes as a man of business, but it seems to me that it is safe enough to put the management of his own—

what used to be his own—place into his hands.
He will have every inducement to care for it.
And if it will make Nita happy, why should
I refuse her that happiness simply because the
man has no money ? He is steady and honest,
that seems certain. I've taken the trouble
and the precaution to find out all about his
college career, and his habits there. It's all
quite satisfactory—less backbone than I could
have wished in my girl's husband, but no
vice ; music and painting and æsthetics—Nita
likes that sort of thing. Do you think I am
a great fool ?'

'I think you are behaving in a very natural
and very sensible manner,' said John. 'He
seems to me to be all you say ; and if he only
makes Nita happy, what more is needed ?'

'Exactly what I think,' said Mr. Bolton.
'Now, leave your books and come and have
supper with us. We haven't seen as much of
you as we ought to have done.'

John shut up the great folio book on ornithology which he had been studying when Mr. Bolton arrived, and picked up some water-colour drawings of different wild birds which lay beside the book. They were exquisitely finished, and, as one could see, copied by a faithful and loving hand, from nature.

'I promised these things to Nita,' he casually observed. ' Perhaps she won't care much about them now. But I will take them, at any rate.'

Mr. Bolton picked them up and looked at them.

' They are very nice,' he observed. ' I wish some other people had such innocent tastes and habits, and would confine their studies to natural objects like these.'

John laughed, a little sarcastically, as he put away his book, and taking the sketches in his hand announced that he was ready.

' When Nita is married—or if she marries, Jack, you'll have to look out for a wife yourself,' observed Mr. Bolton.

'Perhaps Nita will look out for some one, then, and do the courting for me,' said John, drily. 'I have no mind to begin it on my own account—and am not likely to find favour if I did.'

'There you talk rubbish, despite that sage head of yours,' replied his elderly friend. 'Suppose you delegate the choice to my cousin ; she has a wonderfully good opinion of you.'

John laughed aloud. 'If her opinion of me is so high, it might be a dangerous thing to confide the choice to her,' he remarked.

'She might take a fancy to Abbot's Knoll, and the master of it !' exclaimed Mr. Bolton, highly delighted. 'There is no accounting for the presumptuous fancies which enter a young man's head. Here we are !'

They had gone in, little suspecting the scene which was even then coming to an end, and the rest of the evening had been passed as has been related.

Jerome naturally knew nothing of all this

conversation. He went to the Abbey the following morning, and there was an un-pleasantly-suggestive rhyme running in his head as he took his way there—that rhyme which gives the excellent advice :

‘ Be sure you're well off with the old love
Before you are on with the new.’

He found Nita at home, and alone—startled and surprised to see him ; overwhelmed with confusion as the sight of him recalled the scene of last night.

Muttering some incoherent words she would have made her escape, but Jerome stopped her, and taking her hands, looked into her face with an expression of such intense gravity, even severity, that she gazed up at him spell-bound and fascinated.

‘ Did your father say anything to you this morning about me ?’ he asked.

‘ No,’ whispered Nita. ‘ Why—what—he

has not told you to go away—oh, he has no told you that ?'

' No. We were talking about you last night, Nita, and he told me this, that if you would marry me, I might stay; but if not, *then* I was to go. What do you say? May I stay? Will you let me try to make you happy, or must I go ?'

Nita was nerveless, cold, and trembling—perhaps never in her life had she felt so unhappy as in this moment—which should have been the one of supreme delight—when the man she loved with all her soul asked her to be his wife.

' Jerome—I—do you mean that you wish this ?' she asked, desperately plunging into the question.

' I mean that I wish it more than anything in the world ; and listen, Nita—I would not conceal this from you—that I have loved, and loved deeply, before ever I knew you : but that is all over, gone, done with, finished !

I cannot offer you all the passion of a first strong love, but I can offer you my life's devotion, if you will be so good, so wonderfully good, as to take it.'

He saw the blank shade that came over her face : he believed that she was going to summon up her strength of will to refuse him. If she did, what was left to him—what in this world to make life worth an hour's living ?

'Nita!' he pleaded, in dire and dreadful earnest; 'for God's sake think before you speak! Do not cast me away! Try to bear with me—or—or—I shall be the most miserable wretch that ever lived !'

There was passion—there was even anguish in his tone—emotions which Nita read there, and which overpowered her. All her love, all her self-abnegation rushed out to meet him :

'Oh, Jerome, if you care for my love—if it will give you one hour's comfort—it is yours, it is yours! And my whole life with it—for I love you better than you can ever know.'

'Better than I can ever deserve, try as I may,' he murmured, in the deep tone of conviction, as he folded her in his arms, and soothed the passionate agitation which shook her—and tried to quench the tears which rushed from her eyes—tears which none could have named with certainty as being of joy or of grief.

But the die was cast: the bargain was struck. He might return to his home with a mind free of care for the future ; but with all the diviner elements in his nature degraded, soiled, maimed, for they had been dragged through the dust, and grievously maltreated.

Avice and her escorts arrived late that afternoon, and he met them, and they went with him to his house. That is, Avice and Ellen went with him—Somerville returned to Brentwood.

Avice felt a chill dismay strike her heart, at her brother's reception of her. There was an absence, a constraint, a coldness in all his words and movements, which would not be removed. She expressed her delight at the sight of her new home, and he absently replied that it was very well, but rather dreary. She felt very soon that some miserable explanation was to come. It came almost directly. They had got into the house, and Avice had taken off her things, and was somewhat languidly partaking of the meal which had been placed before her. Suddenly she said :

'Jerome, you have never once asked after Sara.'

She saw his face suddenly turn pale, and his lips set. The hand which had been lying on the table, trifling with a paper-knife, closed upon that knife quickly and firmly : he raised his eyes to his sister's face, and said coldly :

' Miss Ford—how is she ?'

' Miss Ford !' ejaculated the young girl, horror-struck. ' Jerome ! what has happened ? You speak as if she was nothing to you.'

' Nor is she anything to me now,' he answered, with that cold and pitiless cruelty, unbending and unremorseful, which so often appears in weak natures when they are driven to choose between themselves and another—when the moment comes in which egoistic or altruistic feelings can no longer be evenly balanced—in which one set must prevail over the other.

' Sara—nothing to you ! I—I do not understand,' she stammered, with a sickening sensation of fear and bewilderment.

' I will explain,' he said, with the same cold glitter in his eyes, his lips drawn to the same thin line—a look she had never seen him wear before, and which sent her heart leaping to her throat.

' For heaven's sake, Jerome, do not look at me in that manner !' she cried. ' It is just

—just as papa used to look when he thought some one wanted punishing.'

' Do not interrupt with such vague, foolish nonsense,' he replied impatiently. ' I am going to write to Miss Ford to-night, to set her free from her engagement to me. And I—wish to be free from her. I am going to marry some one else.'

Avice had pushed back her chair, and sat looking wildly at him ; her hands clenched tightly ; her breath coming quickly, but unable to speak a word.

' It is as well you should understand this,' he said, again beginning to balance the paper-knife. ' To-night you will want to rest, I suppose, but afterwards you will have to meet the lady I speak of ; and it is to be hoped you will conduct yourself with more composure, more self-respect, in fact, than you display at present.'

Then Avice found words.

' Do you imagine that I will be false just

because it pleases you to be so!' she exclaimed. ' If you choose to behave like a
coward and a liar—yes, a coward and a liar,'
she repeated, looking full into his eyes with
an unblenching scorn that scorched him, 'and
that to the noblest woman that ever lived, *I*
am neither a coward nor a liar. I will have
nothing to do with this girl you are going to
marry. You have brought me home, and
you can make me miserable, I suppose. And
you can make me see her, I dare say; but you
can never make me like her, or behave as if
I liked her, or as if I wished her to be my
sister. And I never will. You may take
my word for it. I stand by Sara Ford to
the last, if I had to die for it.'

She spoke with vehement passion, and
looked transformed. She spoke too like a
woman, not like a child any more. And yet
she was but a child, and a helpless one. He
answered composedly :

' It is as well that you have shown me by

this specimen how you intend to behave. I
will give you till to-morrow morning to reflect
upon your position. Allow me to remind
you that I never asked you to behave to
Miss Bolton as if you liked her. It will be
perfectly immaterial to her how you behave.
But I want civility from you towards my
future wife, or, if you choose to withhold it,
I shall have to exert my authority as your
guardian, and remove you—in other words,
my dear little girl, I have no wish to make
your life uncomfortable, but unless you can
obey me without making scenes like this, I
shall send you to school.'

Now ' school' had been the horror, and the
bugbear, and the *bête noire* of Miss Wellfield's
life from her earliest childhood. She had
often been threatened with it; and seldom
had the threat failed to work its soothing
spell. On hearing Jerome's words now—on
seeing the cool unrelenting expression in his
eyes, and the slight sarcastic smile upon his

lips, and recognising the absolute power he
held over her destiny—how easily he could
make her miserable, if not so easily happy;
remembering that Sara was far away, and
that under the circumstances she might never
see that dear friend again ; remembering that
she had never seen this Miss Bolton, who
might be quite ignorant of all that had happened—remembering, in short, her own help-
lessness and desolation, she burst into a
passion of tears, of hopeless, agonised weeping, exclaiming now and then :

‘ What a home-coming ! Oh, what a dreadful coming home !’

Jerome let her cry in the corner of the
settee, and took no notice of her; till about
seven o'clock he rose from his chair, went to
her and put his hand upon her shoulder.
She looked up, her face all tear-stained and
pitiful ; her golden hair tumbled about her
head.

‘ I am going to the Abbey, and shall not be

in till after ten o'clock,' he said. 'Am I to
tell Miss Bolton that I may take you to see
her to-morrow, or not ?'

'I don't know,' replied Avice, hopelessly.

'Ah, you will know by to-morrow. I shall
tell her that I intend to bring you. Good-
evening. I should advise you to go to bed
before long.'

But she did not go to bed. She sat in a
stupor of grief and bewilderment. While
she had been crying, Jerome had written a
letter. Her passion had irritated him, and
he had allowed his irritation to influence his
words to Sara. He had 'set her free' (no
need to put such a pitiful document into
print—it was feeble and despicable, illogical,
and yet stabbing like a dagger, as such pro-
ductions—the efforts of selfishness to kick
down the ladder by which it has risen—
always must be). 'He would not stand in
her way, he who had nothing to offer her—
no faintest prospect of a home, or of anything

4—2

worthy to give her.' In short, under the pretence of consulting her interests, Jerome Wellfield very decidedly asked Sara Ford to dismiss him, to release him from his bond.

Avice, of course, knew nothing of this. She only knew that she had come home to find everything miserable, to find an impostor in the brother to whom she had given the whole worship of her youthful heart. And yet, was he an impostor, or was he not rather a very wicked, dark, bad man, like some Byronic hero ?

She sat in the corner of the settee, darkly brooding, when some one tapped quickly at the front door; and then she heard it open, and a man's step in the little porch. Some one entered, saying in a slow, lazy voice :

'I say, Wellfield, I thought I'd call to wish—— Oh, I beg your pardon !' followed in a more animated accent.

Avice looked at the speaker, and saw a tall, clumsy-looking young man peering at

her, rather than looking, from a pair of short-
sighted brown eyes. On his homely, square-
cut face there was an expression of some em-
barrassment, not partaken of in the least by
Miss Wellfield. She rose, made a gracious
bow, mentally casting a reflection of some
dismay upon her probably dishevelled appearance, and said, with self-possession :

'My brother has gone to the Abbey.'

To herself she was thinking, 'What a
great, queer, awkward-looking creature.
Surely *he* can't belong to one of those "fossi-
lised Roman Catholic families" whom Jerome
told me about, as being the only aborigines
fit to visit.'

'Oh ! I saw the light in the window, and
supposed he was in. I did not know you had
arrived.'

'Do you want to see him particularly ?'

'Oh, another time will do, I suppose. He
has just got engaged to my cousin and my
greatest friend, and I came to wish him joy.'

A pause. Then Avice said :

'Miss Bolton is your cousin. Then of course you know her ?'

'I have known her since she was a baby.'

'Then you must be Mr. Leyburn, I am sure. Jerome often used to speak of you in his letters.' .

'Yes, that is my name,' said John, unable to take his eyes from the figure before him, with her lovely flushed face, ruffled golden hair, and violet eyes at once bright with recent tears and dark and tired with the fatigue of travelling, and, it must be confessed, with an overpowering drowsiness, to which she had been just on the point of yielding when he arrived. She was like nothing he had ever seen before, and he felt tongue-tied and paralysed in her presence—as if, if he spoke, he would infallibly say something idiotic, even drivelling, and as though, if he moved, his boots would creak, or he would fall over something. Together with these sensations, an intense anxiety neither to speak as a fool, nor to tumble down ; which combined currents of emotion rendered his position anything but an agreeable one.

Avice herself had begun to think :

' He is fearfully clumsy, but I am sure he has honest eyes; and if he has known this horrid girl all his life, he can tell me something about her. I shall ask him.'

She therefore said :

' I was too tired to go out to-night, and——'

'And I am keeping you,' exclaimed John, hastily, shocked at the reflections called up by this discovery.

' Not at all. I wish you would tell me something about Miss Bolton, as you know her so well. Is she pretty ?'

John looked involuntarily at the lovely face and form confronting him, and replied, slowly:

' Not very—but she is a perfect angel of goodness, and very nice.'

'Ah!' said Avice, looking earnestly at him, while a new element seemed introduced into the complication. If Miss Bolton was good and nice, it was not Sara Ford alone who had been wronged.

'Is she clever?' she pursued.

'She may not be exactly a genius,' said John, 'but she is the very least stupid girl I ever knew. She is charming. I—I should think you would like her,' he added, a little confusedly.

'It is to be hoped I may, as she is to be my brother's wife,' said Avice, in so sharp and bitter a tone that John looked at her in astonishment. Avice saw the look, and said hastily : 'The engagement is a surprise to me. I only heard of it this evening.'

'Because it was only decided this morning,' said John, with a beaming smile. 'Nita only told me of it herself this afternoon. I've been congratulating her, and it is good to see her so happy. And I think I shall pursue Well-

field up to the Abbey, and give him my good
wishes there. Nita will not mind. Good-
night, Miss Wellfield.'

John's drawl saved his sentences from the
appearance of abruptness which might otherwise have marred their beauty.

' Good-night,' said Avice, absently.

She held out her hand, and he shook it,
and then let himself out, painfully conscious
that he knocked his feet together, and dashed
an umbrella or two to the ground in his exit,
in a manner of which Wellfield, and such as
he, would never have been guilty.

As for Avice, she was reflecting more and
more hopelessly on the situation. Good,
clever, charming, and very happy. Then it
was evident that she loved Jerome very
much—and if she knew nothing, it was not
she who was to blame.

Avice carried her meditations to her room,
where weariness soon overcame her. In
sleep she forgot alike the long journey home,

the strange, cold reception accorded to her, the dreadful news Jerome had given her, her own anguish, and the great wrong done to Sara Ford. She forgot even to wonder whether she should consent to go and see Miss Bolton the following day, or sternly choose a dreary fate, and, for the sake of duty, go to school.

CHAPTER IV.

ITH the morning, when Jerome asked her what she was going to do, Avice replied :

'The only thing, there is for me to do I suppose. I must go and see her, since you insist upon it.'

The flash in her eyes, as she spoke, was as far removed from meekness as anything well could be. Jerome recognised, he could not help it, traces of Sara's influence—of her free, grand, bold nature in his quiet little sister.

With Sara no good quality was suppressed, and he had noticed, even yesterday, a franker, freer, more open bearing in his sister. It was disagreeably apparent again to-day, because, of course, independent outspokenness must be inconvenient and irksome to a selfishness which has had to descend to subterfuge and intrigue, and the conscience of which is no longer a 'flawless crystal.' Yes, he recognised the broad, bold seal of Sara's soul stamped upon this fragile-looking girl.

'I am glad you have begun to think and speak more reasonably,' he said coolly.

'I do not think any differently,' she flashed out. 'I think exactly the same; but I have heard things about Miss Bolton which make me think that I ought to pity her, not hate her; and I shall be silent about you and what you have done, because I believe it will be for the best—not because I agree with you.'

'I shall be in to lunch at half-past one,' he said, 'and afterwards we can go up to the Abbey.'

He could not answer her, but he could not

silence her, and his feelings were not enviable. Avice, he perceived had the whip-like tongue of her father, only with her the whip was used to scourge all that was not 'pure and of good report.'

'Very well,' she replied, indifferently. 'I shall probably go and see Ellen off to the station, and after that I shall remain indoors.'

'Ellen!' he exclaimed, for he had forgotten her. He went into the kitchen, and gave her the letter which she carried to Sara Ford. He could not meet the woman's eyes; he could not look either easy, or natural, or self-possessed, as he desired her to give the letter, without adding word or message. He perceived, without looking at her, that she held herself stiffly, and received the envelope and his commission in perfect silence. Then he went into the parlour again, and had taken his hat off the peg, when Avice called out in a voice from which all the liquid tenderness of their first acquaintance had vanished:

' Jerome, is it permitted me to write to my friend Miss Ford ?'

He turned back upon her with scintillating eyes, and teeth set.

' Avice, take care how you go too far,' he said.

But there was not a drop of craven blood in her veins. There was dauntless defiance in her open glance, as she said :

' Surely you never wish me to speak of her as *your* friend again ! And I merely ask to hear what you have to say, because I intend to write whatever your answer may be. I wished to take precautions—that's all. I intend, metaphorically, to cast myself at her feet, and beg her not to visit the sins of my brother too hardly upon me.'

' Since you have made up your mind what to do, it was unnecessary to ask me,' he answered, setting his teeth.

' I take that as a most gracious permission. I am glad that you see and speak more reasonably,' she retorted, mocking his own words.

He did not speak, but left the house, and during his short journey to the station he felt —it was a degrading feeling, no doubt—but he, Jerome Wellfield, who, six months ago, had been as proud, as fastidious, and as exclusive a young man as any one of them that trod this earth, crouched morally at that moment, like a whipped hound. He was conscious of a cowardly longing to make Avice and Nita known to one another as speedily as possible. He had an intuitive conviction that Nita's charm would soon win Avice's heart, and then his mistress's purity and sweetness would stand between him and his sister's tongue. It was a delightful, an elevating, a soul-inspiring position, and he enjoyed it to the full.

Avice, left behind, broke down, burst into a passion of tears, and, engrossed in her sorrow, was surprised by Ellen, who was

going away. To her she gave the broken
messages which Ellen had repeated to her
mistress. She was in too sore distress to go
with Mrs. Nelson to the station ; but parted
from her with more floods of tears, and cried
long after she had gone, till she had a headache, and everything looked blurred and dim
before her eyes, and while she was in this
condition some one knocked at the door, and
on the servant opening it, Avice heard a soft,
gentle voice ask if Miss Wellfield was at
home, and the answer in the affirmative of
the country servant, who would have said
the same thing had Avice been fainting, or
raving in a delirium. No escape was possible, for the front-door of the old house
opened, as has been said, straight into the
irregular-shaped, raftered parlour.

She gazed earnestly at the figure of the girl
who now entered, with a great dun-coloured
mastiff at her side, whose demeanour pro-
claimed him an inseparable companion. She

saw a slight, pretty figure in a large sealskin
paletot and a shady velvet hat with a large
black feather drooping round the brim, and
soft-hued brown velvet dress. Compared
with the splendid beauty and queenly presence
of that other woman this was an insignificant
apparition enough, but Avice's eye and heart
instantly appreciated the charm of the sym-
pathetic eyes, the mobile face, and gentle
manner.

Nita came forward, looking like anything
rather than a rich heiress who had just
triumphantly bought away by her gold the
allegiance of another woman's lover—which
was the character in which Avice had pictured her to herself: it was she who was
blushing and embarrassed, and who said,
almost timidly:

' I could not wait till afternoon to see you ;
and I did not like Jerome to bring you up to
the Abbey to me, as if I were some one so
dreadfully grand. I thought we could get on

better without him'—she smiled—'and I hope
you don't mind my having come.'

She held out her hand. Avice was overpowered. With all her wrath and indignation
she was but a soft-hearted girl. The instant
she saw Nita she comprehended that it was
she who had been deceived all along. She
felt she could not hate this girl, even to remain
loyal to Sara Ford. She stood still and
silent, with a quivering lip. Nita saw it, and
took both her hands, saying :

'I hope you don't mind. I will go away if
you do.'

'No—no. It is very kind—very good of
you to come,' said Avice, her voice dying
away ; breaking down entirely, she wept
again, as she realised the miserable hope-
lessness of the whole affair.

'What is the matter ?' said Nita, sitting
down beside her. 'Why do you cry ? Is it
because Jerome has asked me to marry him ?
I hope not ?'

'It—it is because I have left a very dear friend,' Avice stammered, and then, with a huge effort, she recovered herself. It would not do—she must be composed.

'Ah, that is sad. But do try not to be too sorry. I hope you will be my friend. I have so longed to see you, and I have asked so many questions about you that I am sure Jerome must have been weary of answering them.'

('"Jerome" at every other word,' thought Avice. 'I am sure she must be desperately fond of him. It is dreadful.')

She recovered herself, lifted her head, dried her eyes, and smiled valiantly.

'I'm very stupid,' she said.

She could not address words of welcome to Nita, and the latter noticed it, but was resolved to ignore it, and to make her new sister love her sooner or later.

'What a beautiful dog you have!' said Avice, stooping to caress him.

'That is Speedwell—my greatest friend,

next to John Leyburn. By the way, John
said he had disturbed you last night, and he
feared you would think him rude.’

‘ I thought him funny,’ said Avice, a small
smile beginning to creep to the corners of her
mouth. Nita sat and looked at her, and suddenly exclaimed :

‘ How beautiful you are ! I always thought
no one could be handsomer than Jerome, but
you are like him—“ only more so,” as John
says. I hope you won’t think me rude if I
look at you rather often.’

This kind of innocent flattery was very
pleasant. Avice began to cheer up, to forget
Ellen on her way to Sara with that dreadful
letter. An hour’s conversation made the girls
like one another thoroughly. Nita was not
satisfied until she had carried Avice off to the
Abbey, and left a message for Jerome, desiring
him, if he wanted either of them, to come
and seek them there.

Here Avice was solemnly introduced to

Mr. Bolton and to Aunt Margaret ; and in observing the latter found such keen entertainment as to make her forget her troubles. It was only when suddenly Jerome stood before them, and she saw him kiss Nita, and the quick, enraptured smile of the latter, that the pain suddenly returned for a moment ; and the thought of Sara, alone, gave her a bitter pang.

John Leyburn joined the party at supper, and was observed to be unusually silent ; in fact, almost speechless. When Nita, being apart with him during the evening, innocently observed :

'What do you think of her, John ? is she not *lovely* ?' the unhappy young man blushed crimson, and, not looking at 'her' at all, fumbled wildly amongst some books, and stammered :

'She's—yes, she's—rather good-looking.'

'John !' exclaimed Nita, looking at him for a moment, and then breaking into laughter,

not loud but prolonged, and of intense enjoyment.

'Well?' said John, maddened in the consciousness that he had said the very thing he
least wished to express; 'rather good-looking'
being the very last description he would have
wished to apply to Avice Wellfield.

The evening passed over. As Jerome and
his sister walked home, he did not ask her
what she thought of Nita, and she did not
volunteer any observation on the subject.
Only, as she held out her hand and wished
him good-night, he asked :

'Well, have you decided whether you will
stay with me, or go to school ?'

She replied, coldly,

'I should prefer to stay here,' and left him.

Indeed, she had quite decided that she
would prefer to stay there. Avice had to
learn early to decide in a difficult matter :
she found herself face to face with a hard
problem; she acted as a girl, as one inex-

perienced and untried, with no great range of observation, no extensive data to go upon, was likely to act. She was conscious that Jerome had done wrong ; she was aware that Sara Ford, at least, must be suffering cruelly from his wrong-doing, and the problem was, whether she ought to tell Nita Bolton what she knew, or whether she ought not to tell her. She ended by not telling her; it seemed enough that there should be one heartbreak in the case. Nita's joy in her love, her happiness, her high spirits, smote upon the other girl's heart many a time during the short engagement that lasted only while settlements were being made, and legal affairs settled : she could not find it in her heart to smite down that joy and happiness; she could not convince herself that it was right to do so.

Meanwhile, two or three days passed, and then Jerome had news—if news it could be called, wordless and yet eloquent as it was—

of Sara. A small packet arrived one morning, and the label belonging to it was directed in her hand; bold, clear, and legible. He opened it, and found the sapphire hoop he had given her when she had promised to marry him. Nothing else—not a word—not a syllable—but that was enough, and more than enough. It contained his 'freedom,' and her condemnation of him—a condemnation too utter, too strong and intense for words. Wellfield had arrived at that pitch of moral degradation in which he felt relieved rather than otherwise, when the ring was in his keeping again. He had opened the packet at the breakfast-table. Avice saw the ring, and with suave but treacherous sweetness of accent, inquired :

' Is that a present for Miss Bolton ?'

Jerome made no answer. He wished the whole business were over, but he felt no compunction now; no thought of turning back or relenting entered his mind.

The marriage was not to be delayed. They only waited until settlements could be arranged, and in cases like that, settlements are not apt to be tedious affairs. Mr. Bolton (suffice it to say this) acted generously. Both Nita and Jerome were amply provided for during Mr. Bolton's lifetime. At his death they were again to have an access of property, but the great bulk of his estate was so arranged that it should fall to Nita's children, especially to an eldest son, in case there should be one. And there was a stipulation that Wellfield should continue to attend to business in Burnham—at least, during Mr. Bolton's lifetime.

To this Jerome agreed, nothing loth ; for a constant leisure, with no fixed or settled occupation, was a prospect he did not like to contemplate.

Everything ran smoothly—wheels which are oiled with that infallible solution known as ' wealth ' usually do run smoothly. Nita

had lost all her first doubts and fears. Jerome
was an assiduous lover; under the new influence she bloomed into life and vigour, and
something that was very near being beauty.
The sad November closed for her in a blaze
of sunshine. The death of the old year was
to be the birth of her new life ; the entrance
to a long, sun-lighted path, down which she
was to travel for the remainder of her life.
Aunt Margaret's 'croakings' had to cease.
Mr. Bolton daily congratulated himself upon
the success of his experiment ; daily felt that
he had done right in seeking Nita's happiness, not the gratification of whatever ambi-
tion might have underlaid his money-making
diligence of the last twenty years.

On the second of December—her twentieth
birthday — a dank, mournful, sad-looking
morning, with the leaden clouds covering up
the hills, and a raw mist rising from the river
—on this morning Anita Bolton became the
wife of Jerome Wellfield ; Avice and John

officiating as bridesmaid and groomsman, Aunt Margaret as guest, and Mr. Bolton in his natural capacity as father, and giver-away of the bride.

When it came to Nita's turn to say ' I will ' to all the portentous questions asked, Avice saw, with a sudden thrill, and a quick remembrance of all the dark background of this wedding ceremony, how the girl made a perceptible pause, and raising her face, turned it towards her bridegroom, looked directly into his eyes, a full, inquiring glance, and then, with a faint smile, and a little nervous sigh, repeated slowly and deliberately :

' I will.'

It was over. The ring was placed upon Nita's hand ; she walked down the aisle of the quaint old church—grey and hoary with the recollections and the dust of many centuries of the dead—down that aisle she went, Jerome Wellfield's wife.

STAGE V.

CHAPTER I.

SARA.

'For life is not as idle ore,
  But iron dug from central gloom :'
And heated hot with burning fears,
And dipped in baths of hissing tears,
  And battered with the strokes of doom,
    To shape and use.'

ELLEN NELSON had conjured her young lady not to fret, for that there was no man in the world who was worth it. But her words had been spoken into ears made unconscious of their meaning by the heart's agony—and for

answer, Miss Ford had fainted in her old
nurse's arms; or, if not absolutely fainting,
she had been stunned and stupid with despair
and the shock and horror of the blow. But
that merciful unconsciousness did not last long.
Soon she roused again to reality; opening
her eyes, and perplexed at first to account for
the blank dejection she felt—for the throbbing
of her temples, and the aching of her heart.
Then it all rushed over her mind : Ellen's
arrival; her brief, portentous words—the
letter she had brought—Sara started up.

'Ellen, where is the letter I was reading?'

'Never mind the letter, Miss Ford. It
will do you no good to read it.'

'I wish to see it. Give it to me, if you
please.'

Reluctantly, Ellen was obliged to yield up
the hated scrap of paper, which her mistress
read through again, with a calm and unmoved
countenance. Then she took off Jerome's
ring, and with hands that were now as steady

as need be, made it up into a little parcel,
directed it, and said :

'Ellen, I am very sorry to send you out
again, so tired as you are; but if you love me,
you must go and put this in the post for me
—get it registered, or whatever it needs—I
don't know. There is a quarter of an hour.
I dare not trust it to anyone else.'

'Surely I will, ma'am, this moment. And
. . . you won't be working yourself into a
state again, while I am out ?'

'Certainly not. Why should I ? That
packet that you hold in your hand—when it
is safely gone, I shall be at peace.'

' I am glad of it, ma'am,' said Ellen, taking
the letter, and hastening as quickly as she
might, to and from the Post-Office.

On her return she found that her young
lady had indeed not been idle. One end of
the table was spread with a cloth, and she had
placed upon it bread and butter, and cold
meat. The gas-stand was lighted, and the

little kettle upon it was singing cheerily—
everything looked bright and cheerful, only
that Miss Ford's face was white and haggard,
and her eyes hollow, while just between her
eyebrows there was a slight fold, telling of a
world of mental suffering.

'Miss Ford!' exclaimed Ellen, almost
shocked; 'you shouldn't have done that. I
could have got my supper ready without so
much trouble.'

'Come, sit down and refresh yourself, Ellen,
for I am sure you will be tired,' said Sara,
composedly. And she insisted upon Ellen's
sitting down, and eating and drinking, while
she asked little questions about England,
sitting upright in her chair, and even laughing
once or twice, but always with the same
blanched face, the same unnatural fixity of
the eyes; and once Ellen saw how, in a
momentary silence, a visible shudder shook
her—how she caught her breath and bit her
lips.

All this took away Ellen's appetite. She scarcly ate anything, but professed herself mightily refreshed with what she had taken ; and then she rose and began to take away the things, and suggested that it was time Miss Ford had her supper too.

'I don't want anything, thank you,' she said ; and it was in vain that Ellen urged her to take something—a glass of wine ; a bit of bread—for she dreaded the results of a long fast and a long vigil, coming upon this present mental and moral anguish.

Sara refused, and there was that in her manner, with all its gentleness, which prevented Ellen from approaching a step nearer. She could only grieve silently, and wish intensely that her young lady had a single friend to whom to turn in this emergency. But there was no one, neither father nor mother nor brother, to help her with sympathising heart and strong protecting hand. There was no one but Ellen herself, and her mental attitude towards the girl always was and had been one of deference, with all the motherly love she felt towards her. Amongst Miss Ford's various friends and acquaintances at Elberthal, she could think only of one whose face had impressed her, whose manner and—to use the expressive German word—whose whole *Wesen* had carried to her mind the conviction that he was trustworthy—and that was Rudolf Falkenberg. But he was, so far as she knew, a new friend, and a man; not one who could be appealed to in such a case. Thus, nothing remained to the poor woman but, when her mistress insisted upon it, to go to bed. She did so, on receiving from Sara a promise that she also would not be long in seeking her room.

Wearied with five days' almost incessant travelling, and exhausted with the mingled emotions which had filled the last forty-eight hours, Ellen, though she had determined not to rest till her mistress went to bed, was soon

overcome with her fatigue, and dropped
asleep; nor did she awaken again until daylight, pouring into her room, told her it must
be growing late. She sprang up, and throwing on a dressing-gown, opened the door and
looked into the parlour. No one was there,
and all was still. Perhaps Sara slept. Ellen
knocked at the closed door of the bedroom,
and was bidden by a ˻composed but weary
voice to come in. She entered, and saw that
Sara had never undressed. She had thrown
a wrapping gown about her, and was just
then seated on a chair beside her bed, which,
as Ellen saw with dismay, had not been disturbed. As the woman entered Sara looked
at her—her face whiter than ever, her eyes
distended, an expression of such blank, utter
woe in her whole look and attitude as appalled
Ellen, who said in a trembling tone :

‘ Child, you promised me to rest !’

‘ Did I, Ellen ?   Then I forgot it, and if I
had remembered, I could not have kept my

promise. I could not have lain still for two seconds.'

'But, Miss Sara, you'll make yourself very ill, and you will break my heart.'

'Oh, what nonsense !' she said, with a sound like a little laugh. 'What is the use of lying down when one can't sleep. By-and by I shall be so tired that I can't help sleeping, and when I feel like that, I will go to bed.'

She folded her hands, and leaned back her head, and there was the same expression upon her face as that which had been there ever since she had given Ellen the little parcel containing Jerome's ring to post—an expression like the changeless one of some beautiful marble mask from which a pair of restless, wretched human eyes looked forth, haunting all who can read the language they speak.

Fear seized Ellen's heart at the long duration of this strained, unnatural calm. She dreaded the end of it. A terrible vision of her young mistress, with perhaps reason for ever overturned, leading an existence worse than death, occurred to her.

'I wish he could see her,' she thought bitterly. 'It would haunt him to his dying day, and if it drove him mad, it is only what he would deserve. To think of an empty fool like that playing with the heart of a woman like this. 'Tis enough to make one believe there's nothing but evil to prevail in the world.'

She dressed herself hastily, and prepared some coffee, of which she induced Sara to partake. The day dragged on. No one came near. Even Falkenberg failed in his usual call. Sara said nothing to Ellen of any suffering she endured. The woman could only guess from the utter transformation of her usual ways and habits that she was enduring tortures, and her own pain and perplexity increased. Once Sara went to her studio, and began to paint; but in a moment she flung down brush and palette, and began to pace about the bare boards, restlessly.

She did not resume the effort : it had been in the first instance mechanical.

The day appeared like a week to Ellen. It was November, when the daylight soon faded. The weather was cold ; there was a foretaste already of a biting winter, in a sharp, black frost, and a leaden sky, which caused the day to close in even earlier than usual.

It was evening. Sara had taken up a book, and was gazing unseeingly at the page, and turning over the leaves restlessly. Suddenly she closed the book, and said :

' Is not this Wednesday, Ellen ?'

' Yes, Miss Sara, it is.'

' It is Frau Wilhelmi's evening at home. I shall go. And if I do, it is time to get ready at once. Will you just go and get my dress ?'

' Miss Ford ! you are not fit to go out,'

exclaimed Ellen, desperation lending boldness to her.

Sara looked at her, and repeated her order. Ellen, in distress, asked which dress she would wear.

'Oh, any. The old black velvet—that will be best, for it is cold.'

Ellen was perforce obliged to go and get out the dress, and help Sara to make her toilette, feeling all the time that it was as if she attired a ghost. When she was ready the young lady looked beautiful, as usual, but it was with a kind of beauty which no sane person cares to see. Face and lips were ghastly white; there was a deathlike composure and calm in her expression; only those beautiful eyes looked restlessly forth, dark and clouded, and full of a misery which surpassed the power of words to utter, or tears to alleviate. Sara hardly knew herself why she was going out; there was a vague consciousness that her own thoughts and the

horrible suffering they brought with them
were becoming rapidly intolerable ; that soon,
if she did not see and speak to some other
beings, she would shriek aloud, or lose her
reason, or that something terrible would
happen. She looked at herself in the glass,
and Ellen suggested that she wanted a little
rouge.

'Rouge!' repeated Sara, laughing drily ;
'why, I am in a fever. Feel my hand!'

Ellen took it, and incidentally felt as well,
while her finger rested on Miss Ford's wrist,
that her pulse was beating with an abnormal
rapidity. But the hand was burning as she
had said.

With a dark foreboding of evil, Ellen
threw a cloak around the girl's shoulders, and
put on her own shawl and bonnet to accompany her, for the Wilhelmi's house was hard
by, and at Elberthal it was the custom to
walk to every kind of entertainment.

'Oh, how cool and refreshing!' exclaimed

Sara with a deep sigh, as the icy air struck upon her burning face.

Ellen's reply was a shiver. They soon stood at the Wilhelmis' door, and, as Ellen left her, Sara bade her return for her at half-past ten. It was then after half-past eight.

The door was opened. Ellen watched her mistress as she passed into the blaze of light in the hall, and, standing there, unfastened her cloak. Then the door was closed again. Repressing her forebodings as well as she could, Ellen returned home, and set herself to counting the minutes until it should be time for her to return to Professor Wilhelmi's.

CHAPTER II.

' YES.'

' And I was a full-leav'd, full-bough'd tree,
  Tranquil and trembling and deep in the night.
And tall and still, down the garden-ways,
  She moved in the liquid, calm moonlight.

' Her moonshot eyes, strained back with grief,
  Her hands clench'd down, she pressed from sight ;
And I was a full-leav'd, full-bough'd tree,
  Tranquil and trembling and deep in the night.'

SARA laid her cloak on a table, and followed the servant into Frau Wilhelmi's reception-room. The well-known scene smote upon her eyes with a weird strangeness and sense of unfamiliarity ; it was the same, with the accustomed sounds of loud talking, merry laughter, and resound-

ing music. Light and sounds blended together and beat upon her brain in a combined thunder. She could distinguish nothing
clearly or distinctly, beyond the faces and the
voices of those who actually came up to her
and addressed her.

By a vast effort of will she kept her composed, impassive demeanour. When she set
out she had a vague idea that on finding herself in the midst of a gay and animated
company, she would be able to smile and
speak and do as they did, even if mechanically. But the effort failed. Her lips felt
stiffened, her tongue tied, so that smiling was
impossible, and only the merest 'Yes' and
'No' would pass her lips.

'*Nun*, Miss Ford!' exclaimed Frau
Wilhelmi, taking her hand. 'You look ill,
recht elend und leidend. Have you got a
cold ?'

'No—a little headache. I thought it

would do me good to come out,' she murmured.

Had she followed her own impulse, she would have turned and left the house again instantly, but she had an underlying determination to go through with the ordeal, having once braved it, albeit it proved more scathing than she had expected.

Then Luise came up to her, laughing, with some absurd story, to which Sara listened, thankful that she was not expected to speak—interruptions being received unfavourably by the volatile Luise. Luise did not notice Miss Ford's excessive pallor, or if she did was too absorbed in her own affairs to observe it particularly, or be shocked by it.

Then came Max Helmuth, who saw instantly that something was wrong, but did not feel himself on sufficiently intimate terms with Miss Ford to ask any questions.

To Sara, the whole thing continued to grow more and more like a hideous dream. She thought she must have been there an hour, and that she might plead her headache as an excuse, and go away. Looking at a great *Schwarzwälder* which hung against the wall of the hall, she saw that it was just ten minutes since she had entered the house.

The rooms were unusually full that evening, and less notice was taken of her than usual; but several pairs of eyes were fixed upon her in wondering astonishment, and she was collected enough to see it, and to desire more strongly than ever to get away. But a mere trifle prevented her—the idea, namely, of the surprise and pity she would see in Frau Wilhelmi's eyes if she went up to her now ten minutes after her arrival, and took leave. She looked around for a chair, feeling like some hunted creature which would escape, but is paralysed with fear when most it needs all its power of wind and limb.

And as she looked round, some one took her hand, and a voice said:

'Pardon me, Miss Ford—you look ill to-night. Would you like to sit down ?'

It was Rudolf who addressed her. For a moment the horrible strain of the nervous tension under which she was suffering relaxed: as she looked up at him her eyes wavered ; her lips and nostrils fluttered for an instant, and she drew a long breath. The end of her endurance was coming, she felt.

'Yes, please,' she said, in a voice that did not rise above a whisper.

He drew her hand through his arm, saying, 'Let us go to the hall—there is a bench there ;' and as he spoke, he glanced casually and unthinkingly down at the hand which a moment ago his own had covered—at Sara's left hand. She wore a pair of old white-lace mittens—one of the few relics of old prosperity which remained to her, and this allowed her hands and their adornments to be fully seen. As Falkenberg glanced at that hand, he missed something. He paused, as they

passed out ; his eyes leaped to her face, to
her hand ; back to her face again. Sara's eyes
had followed his. The first flush of colour
that had touched her cheeks since Ellen had
brought her message of sorrow, rushed over
her face now. She understood the look, the
glance which asked, ' Your ring—where is it ?'

'Yes,' she said, beneath her breath, and
then, as if mastering a momentary weakness,
she recovered herself ; her face took the
same marble whiteness again. She let him
lead her to a cushioned bench near a pyramid
of ferns and a little fountain, which stood in the
centre of the hall. She sat down, but it was
only for a moment. Then she started up
again, 'Will you—would you mind taking
me home again ? I—I feel ill,' she faltered,
her powers of endurance at an end.

'Surely I will,' he answered, finding her
cloak and wrapping it round her.

Sara gathered up her dress, took his arm,
and they passed out of the house.

Five minutes' walking brought them to the
door of her home. Falkenberg rang the bell,
and as they waited, he said :

'Miss Ford, may I come in ? There is
something I want to say to you.'

'Oh yes ! Come in and say what you
like !' she replied ; and now that she had
found speech again, the impulse to reveal her
agony was uncontrollable—or, rather, the
power of concealing it, of speaking of other
things, had disappeared. 'Say what you like,'
she repeated. ' If you had come to say you
had brought something to kill me with, I
would thank you on my knees.'

' Yes, I know you would, but I have not
brought that,' he answered, as the door
swung open from within, and they entered.

Ellen started up on seeing them.

'Oh, sir, I am glad you have brought Miss
Ford home !' she exclaimed.

'Leave us, Ellen,' said her mistress. 'Herr
Falkenberg wishes to speak with me.'

Ellen left the room. Sara looked at her guest. He, too, was pale, and his eyes full of a deep and serious purpose. His heart, too, was aching, with a pain almost as intolerable as that of her own.

He read the whole story; that which caused his pain was his own powerlessness to help her. He knew her better than she knew herself. He knew that it was not grief which gave the keenest sting to her present agony, but her outraged pride—the blow which had been dealt to her honour and her self-respect. It was upon that feeling that he calculated now, in what he was about to do. It was upon that, that he staked his whole hopes, as he threw. He had told her once that she might, some day, do something which conventional people would call outrageous. He was bent now upon persuading her to such a deed, and he trusted chiefly to that infuriated pride to help him.

' Well ?' she said, with a harsh laugh, ' have

you come to talk about my missing ring,
Herr Falkenberg? Do you want to know
where it is, and who has it now? I can in-
form you that it has gone back to the man
who gave it me—because—because he has
sent me word that I am free. He thinks of
marrying some one else.'

There was a discordant, grating sound in
her voice, and she laughed again. The laugh
encouraged Rudolf in his purpose.

'I guessed it was something like that,' he
said, 'when I saw that it was gone. The
man could neither appreciate nor understand
you. I have felt it for a long time.'

'Is that to console me?' she asked sarcastically.

'It should console you, in time. Women
of such stuff as you are made of cannot grieve
for ever for a coxcomb. If they do, they de-
grade themselves to his level.'

He saw the scarlet colour that rushed over
her face and throat, and the strangely

mingled glance she threw towards him. He had not miscalculated.

' You did not know him. ' You have no right to call him a coxcomb,' she said. ' You slight me by——'

' By supposing you capable of making a mistake ? There you are wrong. The only thing that can be infallibly predicted by one human being of another, is that during his life he will make a great many mistakes. I should slight you if I supposed you capable for a moment of breaking your heart for Jerome Wellfield.'

He had spoken the name advisedly. It had never passed between them before. Its effect was to make her cover her face with her hands, and cry faintly and pitiably.

As Falkenberg saw this sight—saw this girl crouching and weeping, and heartbroken and desperate in consequence of having been deceived and deserted by Jerome Wellfield, his heart was hot within him. He went up to her, took her hands from before her face, and as she looked at him she saw that his eyes were full of wrath, and his brow clouded with angry feeling.

'Sara!' he said abruptly, and almost sharply, 'you demean yourself by this behaviour. Listen to me : answer me : You will never cast a thought to that man again. If he were at your feet to-morrow you would turn away from him, for you are no patient Griseldis. Is not this true ?'

'Of course!' she exclaimed, brokenly; 'why do you ask me such questions? Do you wish to insult me ?'

'No. I only wanted your word for what I felt to be true. Nothing—no repentance on his part would induce you to——'

'I will not bear it,' she exclaimed, passionately. 'Let me go. You have no right to——'

'Sara, I have no right to say any of these things to you. I know it too well. Will

you give me the right—not to ask any more
such questions—but to protect you and stand
by you in this and every other trouble you
may have ? Will you leave Jerome Wellfield
to reap what he has sown, and let me try to
prove to you that there are men left in this
world who know how to set a woman's
happiness higher than their own convenience ?
Will you be my wife ?'

Falkenberg had once or twice tested the
extent of his influence over Sara, but he had
never pushed the experiment so far as this ;
and he felt that it was a crucial test : his
power over her trembled in the balance ;
with her final decision now it must stand or
fall. As she did not speak, but sat still,
gazing at him, while he, stooping towards
her, held her hands, and looked intently into
her face, he went on :

'You have been too absorbed to see that
it was no mere "friendship" I felt for you.
But I tell you now, that I would wait for

you to my life's end—only, I cannot keep up
this show of indifference. Choose now,
Sara. Promise to be my wife, or dismiss
me once for all. It must be one or the
other.'

'Oh, do not leave me here alone!' she
cried, involuntarily.

'Then consent to what I ask. You told
me once that you had faith in me, that you
believed in me. Have you lost it all?'

'Not a jot.'

'Then take my word when I tell you that
you shall not repent. Let me call you my
wife. Give me the duties of your husband;
I ask for no privileges. I will wait—wait
twenty years, and never repent. Neither
shall you.'

'But you know—you must know—I do not
love you. I am not sure that I do not love
him, even yet—may God help me!'

'Yes, I can understand it all. But decide,
Sara, now—at once. Once again I give you

the alternative; it depends on you whether I go or stay.’

This was intimidation, and he knew it. He used it because he had a great end in view, and he saw no other way of gaining it.

‘Speak !’ he added. ‘Do you consent ?’

A long pause, till she answered coldly, and turning, if possible, a shade paler than before :

‘Yes.’

‘I thank you from my very soul,’ he answered, kissing first one and then the other of the cold nerveless hands he held. ‘And now I will leave you. You would prefer to be alone, I know. Good-night ! Remember, all I am and have are at your service.’

She made no answer, and the deathly hue of her face never changed or altered. She did not reply to his good-night, nor take any notice of him, as he went out of the room.

He found Ellen, and sent her into the room, saying :

' I think your mistress will be ill. If she is, send for me. She will quite approve of it.'

Wondering, Ellen went into the sitting-room, and her heart echoed Falkenberg's words when she saw her mistress. Ellen had come to feel that the most utter break-down—fever, delirium, or raving—would be better than this prolonged conscious suffering. She could almost have found it in her heart to pray for death or madness to come and relieve her darling from this torture.

' May he be paid his just wages !' she kept wishing within herself, ' measure for measure —not a grain more or less ; and he'll have had about as much as he can endure. I ask no more.'

The end of that long-drawn agony came at last, as come it must. After Falkenberg had gone, Sara began to pace about the room ; once or twice the consciousness of

what had passed between her and him,
crossed her mind, and a vague accompanying
idea, which scarcely attained the consistency
of a positive intention—that when she was
better, and better able to reason, she would
tell him that she had made a mistake; that
what he bargained for was out of the question; she would do him no such wrong. His
threat of leaving her had been the last straw;
she had been unable to face the alternative.
She could not do without him; for in crises
like these we see every day the adage belied
that 'vain is the help of man.' It is man
alone that can sustain and comfort man in
such an emergency; it is then that there is
brought home to us the utter powerlessness
of supernatural aids to touch our woe.

Ellen, in her room, towards morning, heard
an abrupt pause in the measured footsteps,
and something like a long moaned-out sigh.
She hastened to the other room, and found
that Sara had at last, dressed as she was,

flung herself upon her bed, and lay there motionless.

When Ellen spoke to her she murmured some incoherent words, but it was evident that she did not understand what was said to her.

The woman felt a sensation almost of relief. At last she could take matters into her own hands, and her first step of course was to send for a doctor—a doctor to cure a strange disease. Where are such physicians to be found? and when shall we cease our quest after them? She sent for Falkenberg, too, as he had desired her to do; and she heard what he said to the doctor who had come out of Sara's room, looking grave. Falkenberg asked him what was the matter—was the case a serious one?

The doctor looked from Rudolf to Ellen, and answered by another question:

'Has the young lady any relations? If she has, they should be sent for.'

'I do not know how that may be,' replied
Falkenberg ; 'or whether she would desire
her relations to be sent for, even if she were
in extremity. But she is my promised wife,
and that being the case, I beg you will consider me responsible in every matter that
concerns her.'

The doctor—a grave man—bowed, also
gravely, and said, that that being the case,
he might say that the lady was very
dangerously ill, and before deciding upon
any measures, he would prefer to consult
with his colleague, Dr. Moritz.

'So be it,' replied Falkenberg, repressing
an impatient sigh.

The note was written : the appointment
made for an hour from that time. Leaving
directions for what was necessary to be done
at once, the doctor departed.

'Sir,' said Ellen, turning with some
agitation to Falkenberg, 'excuse me, but is
it true what you said to the doctor, that

my young lady had promised to marry you ?'

'Quite true. I wrung it from her last night, by telling her that she degraded herself by grieving for that other fellow. And if she lives, my friend, I intend her to be my wife; therefore don't distress yourself on the subject. You will keep faith, and are her oldest friend, therefore I wish there to be confidence between us.'

'Thank you, sir. I hope indeed you may succeed. I wish you well with all my heart,' she said.

❋   ❋   ❋   ❋   ❋

The two doctors looked very grave. It was as Ellen had dreaded—they feared for the permanent loss of her reason, after the long, unendurable strain, and the cruel blow she had had. Falkenberg, without naming names, inspired only by an intense desire for her recovery, had judged it best to be tolerably explicit as to facts. One of the doctors—he named Moritz—looked down at the unconscious face, remarking :

'Ay! She has been betrayed, and there are natures to which betrayal is death.'

'But Miss Sara was never one to give way,' said Ellen, appealingly. 'She was as strong as a man, sir, and as simple as a child, in her mind.'

'Then she stands so much the better chance. From what you say I conclude she was not a morbid subject,' he answered, as he went away.

Falkenberg's visits were, of course, daily. Wilhelmi called many times. His wife and daughter went once into the sick-room, and came out again; Frau Wilhelmi with all her mother's heart showing in the pity of her eyes, Luise crying aloud, and vowing that she would never forget it till her dying day. The sight of her proud and beautiful friend tossing senselessly to and fro—of the great grey eyes gazing with meaningless fixity at her—of the vacant stare and smile upon the face that had once beamed with intellect, had shaken her careless girl's heart, and given her a glimpse into depths she had never dreamed of before.

'*Ach*, mamma!' she murmured, as they went sorrowfully away: 'I don't think Falkenberg will ever have his wish—*der Arme!*'

'Who knows?' answered Frau Wilhelmi. 'I am glad her mother cannot see her.'

It was a desperate battle, if not a very long one. For more than a week life and reason in the one balance, death or madness in the other, oscillated with a terrible uncertainty. But Sara Ford was not doomed to lose either life or reason in the struggle. 'Strong light,' says Goethe, 'throws strong shadow.' And a strong, intense nature makes a strong, obstinate struggle against all kinds of adversities which 'the subtlety of the devil or man' may bring about. There came an evening when the doctors, going away, pronounced her *safe*—sane, living, if with no more strength than a two-weeks' child may possess.

It was after they had departed, and while the nurse kept watch over her patient, that Ellen, after literally feasting her eyes upon her 'child's' face, shrunk to a shadow of its former beauty, went into the parlour for a few minutes, to take a moment's rest, and to indulge in the luxury of some thankful tears. It was quite late, yet she was scarcely surprised to suddenly see Herr Falkenberg, who strode into the room, and, standing before her, asked breathlessly :

' Is it true, what I heard outside—that she is *safe* ?'

' It is quite true, sir, I thank God !'

' Oh !' he said, biting his lips, and drawing in his breath with a long inspiration.

The next moment he had cast himself upon a chair beside the table, and, with his

face buried in his hands, was sobbing
aloud.

Awe-struck, Ellen stood by for a few
moments, till he looked up and demanded to
hear every particular of this recovery, this
conquest, this triumph over death, which,
though they had always professed themselves
so sure of it, came upon him at last with a
sense of joy and relief that was almost overwhelming.

' I must see her as soon as she can see or
speak to anyone,' he said. 'You said you
were my friend, Ellen, and you must manage
this for me. If she gets well and strong, she
will try to break off her compact, out of mistaken consideration for me—you understand ?'

Ellen did not understand, but she had an
intense desire to know her mistress Rudolf
Falkenberg's wife, because she was convinced
he was good. She knew, from innumerable
stories, that he was rich, and, in his way, as

great a man as some great nobleman, and
therefore a suitable husband for Miss Ford,
though not at all beyond her claims. But
firstly and chiefly she wished it from a feeling,
vulgar enough, and natural enough too, to
one of her position, up-bringing, and mental
calibre—she wished it as a kind of revenge
upon Jerome Wellfield—to show him that a
man worth a hundred of him in every respect
was only too glad and eager to win the prize
which he had cast aside.

From this motive, if from no other, she
would strain every nerve to forward Falkenberg's cause. Therefore, when he said to her
' You understand?' she affirmed that she
understood perfectly, and so let him go.

CHAPTER III.

ANY days elapsed before Sara was permitted to see anyone. Then, one afternoon, Frau Wilhelmi was allowed to call, and sat for a few moments talking of the most commonplace and least agitating topics. On the afternoon following that, Ellen cautiously began to prepare the way for Falkenberg. As soon as she mentioned his name, her mistress said :

'If Herr Falkenberg calls, I should like to see him.'

This was when she was so far recovered as to be dressed about noon, or one o'clock, and, half carried, half walking, to make a pilgrimage to the couch or *chaise longue* in her parlour, there to remain until the authorities intimated that it was time to go to bed again.

Falkenberg did call, half an hour after those words had passed between Ellen and her mistress. Ellen repeated them to him, and ushered him into the parlour, where Sara lay on the couch, looking infinitely weak and exhausted, and scarcely able to lift a hand, or to smile faintly, when the tall, strong man came softly up to her ; his face working, his eyes dim.

'You have been very good—unspeakably good,' she said weakly, as he bent speechlessly over her hand. 'Ellen has told me of your great goodness,' she added, in a stronger voice.

'There is no goodness—there has been nothing but the pleasure I have felt in gratifying my own wishes,' he said, in a husky, broken voice.

'It is good to see your face again, and to hear your voice, after the Valley of the Shadow of Death,' she replied, her hollow eyes dwelling, with an expression of something like curiosity, upon his face.

'Do not let us speak of that. You are here once more in the light of life—to work, and hope, and make us glad again.'

She shook her head slowly.

'You are far wiser than I am,' she answered, 'so I will not contradict you.'

'But in the meantime, you disagree with me from beginning to end,' he said, regaining his composure gradually. 'You feel that hope and work are over for you.'

'Yes, I feel as if I did not want to see the light of the sun any more.'

'Nor to talk or think about anything again?' he suggested, and his voice trembled; he trembled himself—his heart was in his throat.

'Yes, just so,' was the languid reply.

'And I am here, brutally to disturb and deny that wish of yours. I am here to give you something to think about, and to tell you of something I want you to do.'

'And what is that?'

'When I say I *want* you to do it, that is a poor, inadequate word. I pray and implore you to keep your promise to me, and as soon as may be—to-morrow, or the day after—to become my wife. I have arranged all the preliminaries. In consequence of your serious illness, the usual notice has been dispensed with. I have nothing to do but intimate to the Bürgermeister the day and the hour for the ceremony, and he, or his representative, will come here to perform it.'

'But—but—surely you have reconsidered it?' she said, flushing painfully.

'I have considered it again and again, with the same result always. Mr. Wellfield's marriage is in the *Times* this morning, to Miss Bolton of Wellfield Abbey.'

Sara winced, and he went on :

'The Wilhelmis know. The Professor and the Frau Professorin have promised to act as witnesses.'

'You have told them?' she ejaculated.

'Yes—because I know that *you* are not a person to go back from your word,' he answered steadily, and he knew that he had conquered—whether because she was weak and feeble, and he strong and determined, or from what cause soever—he knew the game was his when she said, slowly :

'You know what people will say of me— that I tried very hard for you, and married you for your money, and so on.'

'*Herrgott!* yes. I know the whole of the jargon they will gabble amongst themselves. Let them, if they like.'

She looked utterly weary, exhausted and worn out. When she spoke her voice was scarce audible. He had to lean towards her to catch the faltering words :

'If I do—will you—settle everything—
no questions — no thinking? *I cannot
think.*'

'You shall hear no more about it until the
Bürgermeister comes to marry us. A few
words then, and the signing of your name,
and all will be over.'

'Very well. Arrange it all as you wish,
and I will do it,' said she, and turned her
head away, and shut her eyes, as if too tired
ever to open them again.

'You shall not repent it. I promise that
you shall not repent it,' he said, carrying her
passive hand to his lips.

Then he left the room. Outside he saw
Mrs. Nelson, and took her aside into Sara's
atelier.

'We shall be married to-morrow, Ellen,' he
observed.

'Thank God, sir! I believe it will be the
saving of my mistress.' She paused, and
added : 'I hope you don't think of separating

us, sir—Miss Ford and me. It would be sorely distressing to us both.'

' Never, while you both live, believe me. I shall have to leave her in your hands for a long time to come yet.'

With that he hastened away, leaving Ellen in a more contented frame of mind than she had enjoyed for a long time.

※   ※   ※   ※   ※

It was afternoon of the following day. Sara was much in the same state—no stronger, no weaker. She saw, with something like apathy, how Wilhelmi, his wife, and Luise came into her room together, spoke to her, and seated themselves side by side.

She had a faint remembrance that Rudolf had said something about witnesses ; she was not quite sure what it all meant, but no doubt it was right. Falkenberg was there too, seated beside her, and, in an unconscious appeal to his protecting power, she had moved her hand into his, and then lay back in her chair, silent and indifferent. He said something to her, an explanation, it seemed, of the circumstances ; something about—

' In cases like this, Sara, they dispense with the usual notice, so there has been no difficulty about getting it done at once.'

She looked rather blankly at him, and in her own mind wondered vaguely what it meant.

Then some strangers entered—the Bürgermeister and his clerk. Words were read. Something was brought to her to sign, which deed, with Rudolf's assistance, she accomplished. Questions were asked as to her age, her name, parentage, and occupation. At each of these she looked helplessly at Falkenberg, or at Ellen, who stood at the other side of her couch. Then more reading ; then a wedding-ring was put upon her finger, and would have rolled off again had not Rudolf caught her hand and held it fast in his.

Then the Bürgermeister and his clerk took

their hats, murmured severally, '*Empfchlc mich zu gnaden,*' bowed to the assembled company, and were gone.

Frau Wilhelmi and Luise came up and kissed her tenderly, and she saw that their eyes were full of tears. Then the Professor came up and took her hand—the good Wilhelmi—and she remembered his generous kindness to her, and smiled what was intended for a grateful smile at him, whereat his eyes too filled with tears, and he too stooped, and kissed her forehead, and said something incoherent about a *gcliebtes Kind,* a *beste Schülerin.*

Then they were all gone, and she was left alone with Ellen and Rudolf. And then Ellen left the room too, while he still sat beside her holding her hand, till at last a little pressure from her fingers caused him to turn and look at her.

She saw that his eyes were moist, and she paused as she beheld the expression upon his

face—the love that transfigured it.   At last
she asked :

'Are we married now ?'

'Yes, we are married.'

'I am afraid I have done you a great wrong
in consenting.'

'Are you ?   It is rather early to begin with
such forebodings.   What makes you think
so ?'

'I feel as if I should never be worth anything again, and that if I were I should not
make you happy.'

'My child, it was not happiness I wanted,
but you, glad or sorry, "loving or loth." Rest
content.   I shall never repent.'

'Promise me that.'

'I promise it fully and freely.'

'Then I am more satisfied.'

'That is all I ask of you.'

They became silent, and he still sat beside
her, her hand locked in his; and as the short
December afternoon closed in, she shut her

eyes, worn out even with this quiet excite-
ment, and he could not tell whether she slept
or not. In the quiet room there was utter
peace and stillness—a wasted, pallid-looking
woman, with eyes wearily closed, and breathing so lightly her bosom scarce seemed to
move; a man watching beside her, whose
strong, calm face never lost its expression of
assured contentment, and whose eyes were
full of peace: surely no very remarkable
scene. But the whole of the gossip-loving
town of Elberthal was ringing with the names
of that man and that woman.

It happened to be Frau Wilhelmi's reception night, and great was the disappointment
felt because neither she, nor her husband, nor
her daughter would enlarge upon the subject
of the marriage they had witnessed that afternoon—would say nothing more than that *if*
Miss Ford recovered, they were sure it would
be an excellent thing.

Max Helmuth found his Luise very sub-

dued, and very tender. No sarcasm and no
coquetries greeted him that night. When he
asked her why she was so quiet, tears filled
her eyes, and she answered :

'Ah, if you knew, *Schatz!* I cannot think
of anything but this afternoon. It was like a
beautiful legend. Do you know that little
picture of papa's, which he shows to very few
people, and then he generally tells them it is
a head of St. Ignatius Loyola ?'

'I know it—yes.'

'Yes. But to me he always calls it " The
Human Face *Divine*," and so it is. Falkenberg
had just the same look this morning, in his
eyes, and on his mouth. When I think of
that, and then hear these wretches gossiping
about it, it makes me feel—I don't know
how. I know I will never talk gossip again,
Max.'

'Till the next time, *Liebchen!* But I hope
Miss Ford will recover, and make him happy,
as he deserves to be.'

CHAPTER IV.

DOUBTS.

'I pray you, is death or birth
The thing that men call so weary?'

THE days of her convalescence passed to Sara like a long, vague dream. Slowly, very slowly, she recovered strength—as if some inner instinct made her unwilling to return to her place amongst that common humanity which had lately dealt her so bitter a blow. December was waning—Christmas was close at hand—before she had gained sufficient strength to walk from one room to the other. That feat was first accomplished with the assistance of Rudolf's

arm. Then she was able to do it alone. It
was after this that she gained strength daily,
and with physical strength also returned
mental strength. She had drifted on, seeing
no visitors save one, and even that one, Rudolf,
had been absent for some days, on the plea
of business. He had left no word as to
when he should return, or what his plans
were.

It was the 22nd of December. Falkenberg
had been absent for five days, and it was now
that doubts and fears began to distress Sara's
soul. For the last few days she had been
reflecting, deeply and uneasily, as Ellen saw,
watching the face she loved. She dreaded
the result of those meditations. Falkenberg's
cause was her cause, and she wished he
would return. But this afternoon she had a
duty to perform, and, seeing Sara sitting lost
in thought, and that thought apparently of
no pleasant nature, she said :

'You look a deal better, ma'am, this

afternoon. Do you think you would be equal
to looking at the letters that have come for
you while you were ill ?'

' Letters ! Are there any letters for me ?'
she demanded eagerly, her whole aspect
changing. ' Bring them at once. Why did
you not tell me before ?'

' The doctor said you had better not have
them, and Herr Falkenberg said I was on no
account to give you them till you were
stronger,' said Ellen, unlocking a drawer, and
taking them out. Her back was turned to
Sara, or she might have seen the sudden start
of the latter at this decided mention of Falkenberg's name, and this close connection of him
and his orders with her and her affairs. Her
colour changed, and she bit her lip. But she
did not speak as Ellen put the letters into
her hand. Her cheek flushed as she turned
them over. There was one with the post-
mark Nassau upon it, and a countess's coronet
on the flap. That was from Frau von

Trockenau. And there was one directed in
Avice Wellfield's hand. Her face changed
as she looked at them, and observed the dates
on the postmarks. They had both been
written lately—the countess's since her marriage, for it was addressed—Sara turned hot
and cold and trembled as she saw the super-
scription—to Frau Rudolf Falkenberg. She
opened this letter first, and read it :

' DEAREST SARA,

' How can I describe the feelings
with which I have heard of the strange things
that have have happened to you—of your
illness (thank God that you are now
restored to us !)—and of your marriage to
Rudolf Falkenberg ? I knew he loved you.
I flatter myself that I was the very first t(
discover how suitable and delightful such'
marriage would be. I can only offer to h^f
of you my most hearty, unmixed congr'
tions. *Ja, ich gratulire vom ganzen* this

und mein Mann auch. I think, if ever there was a noble, generous, good fellow, it is the man you have married. I should say he was perfect if I were speaking to an ordinary person, but I know you agree with me that perfect people must be so very horrid, and it always sounds to me more of an insult than anything else to call a person perfect. But it is a perfect arrangement all the same. How seldom, dear Sara, do we find the ways of Providence exemplified thus clearly and simply—everything working together for good in so palpable a manner that he who runs may read.' [The countess's moral rejections had been wont, in former days, to excite Sara's intense amusement. Even now, ⁊ the tumult of her feelings, she could not ₊p smiling at this specimen of them.] 'It his my heart good—it does indeed. I feel the ₊py as I did myself when I had just been marₐl to Fritz. Write, or get your husband on th as soon as possible, to tell me how

9

soon you will come to see us, and what your
movements arc going to be.   How I long to
see you both!

> ‘ Yours,

> ‘ CARLA VON TROCKENAU.’

Sara drew a long breath as she finished
reading this effusion, and the colour rushed
over her cheeks and brow and throat.   Now,
for the first time, she began to realise what
the step meant that she had taken.

In vain she tried to reassure herself by re-
calling Rudolf’s promise that she should n
repent, and that he would never repent.   Sl
could not be calm ; she could not view
matter indifferently.   She could not rid
self of the idea that she had hurried and
tened to take an irrevocable step ; that
agony of outraged pride and love re
she had promised, and in her after
helpless weakness and weary indiff
had done that which might mar a

life, and make her own even more miserable than she had expected it would be.

What was she to do? How to meet him? When he came she must brace herself to the task of coming to some explanation, and she shrank in anticipation from what must be so intensely painful an interview.

Thus meditating, her eye fell upon Avice's letter. At first she could only look at it, she could not open it. With the sight of that familiar handwriting there came rushing over her mind a vivid recollection of all the past sweetness and bitterness connected with Avice and those belonging to her. There came the recollection of Jerome—a memory which had slumbered since her illness, and which she had never allowed to awaken. Now it sprang forth again, irresistible, strong, and overpowering. Again she felt his influence, recalled to mind the love she had borne him, the—what was this feeling she experienced even now? Surely she did not love him yet? 'No!' cried every voice within her. And yet, beyond them all, was a whisper, more potent than any of them, asking what it was that she felt, demanding to know the meaning of this eager longing, this *Sehnsucht*, this yearning.

'I am sure I have done wrong. I have made a horrible mistake!' she repeated to herself. 'What am I to do? How shall I repair it?'

With an effort she opened Avice's letter, and read it with a throbbing heart. The girl gave a full account of her arrival at home, and of all that had happened since. She implored Sara to remember that she had known nothing of all that was going on, and not to punish her for Jerome's sin. She related how the marriage was over, how Jerome and Nita were away, and she was at the Abbey with Mr. Bolton and Miss Shuttleworth as her companions; how Mr. Bolton was going to live at Monk's Gate, 'when they came home,' but that she, Avice, was to live at the Abbey with 'them.'

With beating heart Sara read Avice's description of Nita, and understood at once that it must have been Wellfield throughout, who had played a double game, and had deceived both the woman he loved, and the woman whom he had married.

This was no case of a vulgar heiress who was anxious to ally herself with a man of old name; it was the case of a very simplehearted loving girl, who had lost her heart irrevocably, and who would evidently suffer as intensely in her way, if not so passionately, as Sara Ford herself had suffered, if ever she knew the truth.

Avice betrayed again and again her liking for her new surroundings—a liking which she uneasily felt that she could not gratify without some disloyalty to her friend. As for Jerome —such had been the revulsion of feeling caused by his conduct, that Avice could not write of him without a certain tinge of bitter sarcasm cropping up through her words ; and more than once occurred a kind of apology for even mentioning his name in a letter to Sara.

' Tell me what to do,' she concluded. ' You have been my guide for so long; I trust you so implicitly that I feel lost without you. Send me one word, Sara, for whatever you say or do must be right.'

' Poor child !' thought her friend, sorrowfully. ' This must be answered at once. I must set her mind at rest. And, I suppose, when I tell her what *I* have done, she will change her opinion as to all I do and say being right. Perhaps it is as well that her illusion should come to an end betimes.'

She determined to make her first essay in letter-writing since her illness, and began by writing that afternoon to Avice and to Frau von Trockenau. To Avice she wrote explaining why she had not been able to

answer her letter earlier. Then she told her
of her marriage, calmly, and in a matter-of
fact way, with the remark that she could not
enter into her reasons for the course she had
taken, and that Avice would probably not
understand them if she did. Of Jerome she
made not the slightest mention, but she
urged Avice to do all in her power to love
and be kind to her sister-in-law. ' From
what you tell me, I am sure she is good. In
being her friend, and doing all you can to
make her happy, you will grow happier
yourself. It is the only thing you can do—
the only right thing, that is.'

She felt that she had at least been right in
urging this upon Avice; and then she wrote
a brief note to Countess Carla, thanking her
for her good wishes, and adding that she
knew absolutely nothing of any plans for the
future—she left everything to Herr Falkenberg; she excused the brevity of her letter
on the plea of illness, and fastened it up.

She had expected to be exhausted by this exertion, but found to her surprise and pleasure that she was less tired than before. Ellen had lighted the lamp, and the room was warm and cheerful. Sara began slowly to pace up and down the room, her thoughts running intently on the letters she had received, and the ideas they had conjured up. Her long, plain dress hung loosely upon the once ample and majestic figure, now wasted to a shadow of its former beauty.

'The loose train of her amber-dropping hair'

was gathered up into a knot upon her neck; there was a faint glow—the harbinger of returning health—upon her wasted cheek. While she thus slowly promenaded to and fro some one knocked at the door.

'*Herein!*' she answered, turning to see who it was, and confronting Rudolf Falkenberg.

She stood suddenly still, colouring highly.

'You did not expect me,' he said, pausing, with the door-handle in his hand. 'Perhaps I intrude!'

There was a look of disappointment in his eyes, which she saw, and made a hasty step forward.

'Indeed you do not. Only this afternoon I was wishing that I could see you, for I have many things to ask you. Please come in,' she added, holding out her hand.

Rudolf took it, and looked at her.

'You are better,' he said. 'You have been writing. I hope you have not been doing too much?'

'No, I assure you I have not. I feel better for it. If you will let me take your arm, I think I could walk about a little longer.'

He gave her his arm, and they paced about for a short time, slowly and in silence.

'I have much to say to you, Herr—I mean Rudolf,' she began.

'Have you ?   I also have something to say to you.   Well ?'

'To-day Ellen gave me my letters.   I had not had them before.'

'And you have answered them at once ?' he said, smiling.   'I like a prompt correspondent.   This augurs well for the future, Sara.'

'I—I wish you to read them,' she said, with a heightened colour.   'Read this of Avice Wellfield's first.'

She gave it to him, and he read it ; then said :

'Poor little girl ! she is in great distress.   Is it allowable to ask what you replied, and whether you intend to keep up the correspondence ?'

'Not if you object in the least,' said Sara, hastily.

'I ?   No.   I would not insult you with such

an objection if you wrote to and heard from her twice a day,' he replied, with a rather proud smile.

'Thank you. And now this from Countess Carla. It has disturbed me very much.'

He read that too, and his countenance also changed.

'This disturbed you—why?' he asked.

Sara withdrew her hand from his arm, and sat down.

'I ought to speak about something,' she faltered; 'about the future. Everyone—all the world knows that I am married to you. I cannot go on living here just as if nothing had happened, and yet——'.

'What business had you to be thinking about things?' he asked, with a half smile. 'Part of the bargain was that I was to do the thinking, as you must remember. You cannot surely suppose that I have let all this time elapse without thinking upon the subject as well?'

'Oh! if you would decide, and tell me what is best, I would so gladly do it!' she exclaimed.

'I have decided everything. The plan is ready, and only waits your approval to be carried out.'

'And what is it? If I could *only* get away from here!'

'You remember Lahnburg, and my house there?'

'Where we spent the day when I was at Nassau? *Mein Genügen*—oh yes, I remember it.'

'You are so much stronger than I had dared to hope or expect, that I think you could bear the journey there at any time almost, if I have a special carriage for you, and take care that you don't get cold. Christmas will be here, you see, directly. To-morrow is the last day before the festivities begin.'

'Yes. And people will come and want to

see me, and I shall not be able to refuse some of them ; and yet it would almost kill me, I think.'

'Of course it would. Well, Lahnburg is a quiet, out-of-the-way place enough. If I took you there to-morrow, and settled you there with Ellen, you would avoid all the bustle here. It is a beautiful place. You don't care to go out, and are not fit for it if you did. I don't think you will find it duller than this, and certainly less painful ; for you will not be under the constraint of feeling that you are known and observed. What do you think ?'

' I should like that,' said Sara, slowly ; and then, after a long pause, she asked in a low voice :

' And you ?'

' I,' replied Falkenberg, with an assumption of indifference, 'oh, I never *live* in the country in. winter. I detest it. Frankfort must be my *Hauptquartier.* My manager is loading me with reproaches for my neglect of money-matters, and I feel there is justice in his complaints. I shall be very much engaged for at least a couple of months to come. I may find time to run over to Lahnburg and see you, once or twice; but you must not expect me to be very attentive. You know,' he concluded, smiling, and glancing at her again, 'six weeks—or, rather, two months ago, I did not suppose I should be married to you, and I made all sorts of engagements, public as well as private—the former at least must be kept. Well, what do you say to my plan ?'

'What do I say?' she repeated, in a voice full of emotion; 'I say that you are too generous, Rudolf, too chivalrous. Believe me, if I had not so lately gone through what I have done, I would offer you more than words of gratitude—I would lay my very life at your feet.'

'Don't agitate yourself; that is forbidden,' he replied, trying to smile with cheerful indifference. Perhaps a ray of hope had inspired him—some faint idea that she might say, 'Are not you also coming to *Mein Genügen?*' If that had been the case, he promptly repressed the feeling, and added :

'All I ask of you is to get well, and try to be contented, *in your own way.* Do not think of me. Perhaps that may come in the future. Nay, do not cry, Sara. I cannot bear to see *that.*'

'Do not scold me. I almost think I begin to see my way now. They say that much is granted to those who watch and pray.'

She spoke the last words half to herself.

'That is true, in a sense, if not literally,' he replied. 'Well, I will see after a carriage to take you by the noon train to-morrow to Lahnburg ; so tell Ellen to have everything ready. Now I must go. I will take your letters, if they are ready.'

Sara wished he would not go at that

moment, but something prevented her from speaking out her wish, and he departed.

'I must be in some wonderful dream,' she repeated to herself, when she was alone. 'It is too wildly impossible to be true. And yet, how well I know that he has been here. He never comes without bringing with him a purer, rarer atmosphere. He looks at things, and tells you how he sees them, and they are never quite the same afterwards. Now with Jerome—Hyperion to——' She paused abruptly, biting her lip, and thinking, 'After all, I never saw which was Hyperion. I have no right to sneer. Shall I ever love him? Surely, at any rate, the remembrance of that other love will wear off enough for me to be able to say to my husband, "Come, let us travel hand in hand at last!" Heaven send it, at least!'

CHAPTER V.

''There is the outside visible progress—the progress which may be seen, striding perceptibly onwards, super-ficial generally, noisy, clamorous—likest to some wild pea, some quickly-growing parasite, blowing brilliantly, and fading rapidly ; there is the inward, invisible progress too—the deep, unseen stream : the plant that grows in darkness, most nourished when all around seems least propitious : it becomes visible in the end—one perfect bloom—beauty crowning beauty—Clytie springs from the sunflower at last, answering the summons of the god.'

T H E journey to Lahnburg was accom-plished in safety. Just before Christmas Eve, with its guests and its letters, its noise and its bustle, arrived, Sara found herself in her new home.

Lahnburg is always a secluded, retired spot, somewhat in the style of ' the world forgetting, by the world forgot ;' and now, in the depth of winter, when tourists had fled, and winds were bleak, it was more silent and quiet than ever. It suited Sara that it should be so— suited all her ideas and wishes.

Yet it was with strange feelings that she found herself again here, on a bleak, sad December afternoon. There was no snow, but the temperature had been falling all day ; a bitter east wind was blowing ; a sullen, leaden sky, against which the body of the cathedral and the rugged shape of the old Heidenthurm showed out black and mournful. The hills looked dark and sad ; the aspect of the whole fair land was changed.

It was about four o'clock in the afternoon when they arrived. Sara, very weary, stayed in her room to rest. When at last she came downstairs, she found the salon empty. There was a large glowing fire in the English open grate; the lamp was turned down; the dancing blazes flickered upon all the objects in the quaint old room, and the first thing that caught Sara's eye was a panel on that old painted spinet on which Falkenberg had been leaning when they were all laughing at the mistake she had made in crediting him with being possessed of a wife and children.

'Where is Herr Falkenberg?' she hastily asked of Ellen, who came in just then.

'He's gone, ma'am. He told me not to disturb you, but to tell you when you came down that he had an engagement at Frank-fort to-night, and he didn't know when he would be able to come over here again, but he would write.'

Sara was silent; her mind filled with various emotions. It was very good of him —what wonderful tact and delicacy he had! and yet, she wished he had left a note be-hind. She wished he had not been so afraid of disturbing her. He might have given her

10—2

the chance of thanking him for his goodness,
and all this provision of luxury and thoughtful care for her comfort and convenience.
But no! It was doubtless best left as it
was. After all, if she had seen him, what
could she have said? So she decided in her
own mind, and ten minutes afterwards was
wondering how soon he would write, and
what he would say when he did so.

    *   *   *   *   *

From this day her life went on in an even
monotonous tenor. In her home, and around
it, was everything that heart could desire in
the way of beauty, of rare and costly things.
The winter proved to be a hard one, and the
old town of Lahnburg lay for months under a
mantle of frost and snow. The air was cold,
clear and keen ; the hills around were white ;
the river flowed black through a plain of spot-
less white ; the skies overhead were generally
of a deep scintillating crystal blue. All
the beauty that winter ever has or can have,

lay around her, and she could enjoy it by going out into her own garden and grounds.

She did not grow happy in the place, nor contented in it, but she grew used to it, and unwilling to move away from it. She grew almost unconsciously to love the deep and profound retirement of it—it was so quiet, so undisturbed, that sometimes she caught herself thinking of 'After life's fitful fever,' and then, with a half-smile, remembering that that applied to death, not life.

Very few persons knew of her being there, save her old friend Countess Carla, who had made a pilgrimage from Nassau, and burst upon her one day unexpectedly, and fortunately alone. She came full of wishes of joy, and of eager congratulations.

Sara—how, she hardly knew, but by a few words far from explicit—managed to convey to the lively little lady something like the true state of the case. The countess was appalled, her face fell, she could hardly speak. At last :

'Sara, there was some one else, you mean.'
Sara assented.

'Was it—do forgive me—but was it Mr.
Wellfield?'

'Yes,' replied Sara, with a voice and a face
like stone.

'*Du mein Himmel!* And—was it from
pique that you married Falkenberg?'

'It was something like that—and because
he made me do it,' said Sara, the anguish
she felt breaking uncontrollably forth in her
trembling voice. 'Don't let us speak of it.
Perhaps it may sometime come right. But
meantime, my dear Carla, don't tell everyone
as if it were the most joyful news imagin-
able.'

'What must you have thought when you
got my letter?' exclaimed the countess.

The little lady looked thoughtful, but
parted from Sara with a tender embrace, and
asked if she might come again, 'quite alone.'

'Oh, if you would!' cried Sara. 'It would

be so kind, and—and I know Rudolf would approve of it.'

' Yes, I have little doubt on that point. I believe I may safely say that he has a high opinion of me,' replied Countess Carla, darting a keen side-glance from under her drooped eyelids at her friend, while she appeared absorbed in fastening her glove.

' Indeed he has !' echoed Sara, fervently.

' Well, we shall be at Trockenau for some little time now, and I will drop you a line to say when I am coming again.'

They parted. Frau von Trockenau shook her head several times as she waited with her servant at the Lahnburg station, for the train to Ems.

' What a complication !' she thought. ' But I am not hopeless. Does she imagine I did not see how she blushed when she informed me that " Rudolf" would approve ?'

Such an odd sound issued at this moment from the lips of the countess that her old man-servant, saluting, advanced a step and said :

'*Zu Befehl, gnädige Frau.*'

'It's nothing, Fritz. I was only laughing at something I was thinking of.'

Frau von Trockenau was the only one of her former friends whom Sara saw in this manner. Of course, in so small a place as Lahnburg, it was soon known that Herr Falkenberg was married, and that his wife was living at present at the old schloss. No doubt there was speculation on the subject, but, if so, it never reached Sara's ears.

She never entered the town, but, as she grew stronger, would take rambles alone, or with Ellen, along the high upland roads which branched off in all directions, at a short distance beyond *Mein Genügen*, and which led by all manner of ways into the interior, across the moors, or through woods and thickets, or between hedges, or straight and poplar-planted, beside the river.

On such excursions they seldom met any but country people and peasants ; rough but civil folk, who were not curious, but who always exchanged greetings—giving her a nod and a ' *Grüss' Euch Gott, gnädige Frau,*' and receiving in exchange a ' *Guten Tag, ich danke,*' from her.

As for Ellen Nelson, her mental attitude was one of some uncertainty. There was a mingling of satisfaction and dissatisfaction. She rejoiced in the changed position of her mistress, in the luxury and lavish plenty of all their surroundings ; she considered that now her beloved child had just what she was entitled to and no more, but she mourned over the incompleteness of a fate which, in the midst of all this outward prosperity, with- held the inward peace which alone could make it enjoyable. Why could not her mistress be herself again ? She liked Avice Wellfield well, but she misliked the letters which so frequently came from her ; the long,

thick letters which Sara read with such
avidity, and which had the effect of giving
brightness to her eye, a flush to her cheek,
new animation to her whole aspect for many
hours after she had received them.   Often,
after such a letter had come, Ellen would
see her lady's lips move as they walked
together—would see her eyes suddenly flash,
or her cheek flush, and all this she misliked ;
nor did she take any more delight in seeing
the letters which Sara always made her post
with her own hand, directed to Miss Wellfield.   Ellen wished that any distraction
might come, in the shape of society, friends,
anything, to divert her mistress's thoughts
from that topic.

   ' She'll never come to think as she ought
of Herr Falkenberg,' the old servant decided
within herself, ' while she can sit here alone
and brood over the past, and have long
letters from Miss Wellfield.   If she would
only take to her painting again, or anything.'

For Sara did not again begin to take to her painting. Of course, for some time the winter weather formed an excuse. It was much too intensely cold to go out taking sketches or painting landscapes. She had once made an attempt, and tried to catch the effect of a crimson and daffodil sunset behind some naked trees, which sunset she could see from one of the side-windows of the salon. But she had not even finished it. There was no life and no pleasure in it.

Ellen fretted, and wished she would begin, little knowing in her ignorance that her lady would have given all she was worth if she could have begun again ; that she had begun to wonder despairingly if all that artistic power in which she had once rejoiced, and concerning which she had been so ambitious, were quenched and gone. It seemed as if those powers had received some paralysing blow. It was in vain that she attempted to resume her art, seeking, with a natural,

healthy impulse after some occupation which
should divert her mind from the things it incessantly dwelt upon. Ellen did not know
how, when one attempt after another had
failed; when she had tried, and no charm,
no interest dawned, nothing but dull, dead,
mechanical strokes, without meaning or inspiration, she had thrown down her palette, and
wept scalding tears of grief and mortification,
wondering bitterly if it were always to be
thus. She read some words one day which
sent a chill to her heart—what if they were
prophetic ?

' Dark the shrine, and dumb the fount of song thence
        welling,
    Save for words more sad than tears of blood, which
        said :
Tell the King, on earth has fallen the glorious dwelling,
    And the water springs which spake, are quenched and
        dead.
Not a cell is left the god, no roof, no cover.
    In his hand the prophet-laurel flowers no more.'

Thus the winter slowly passed away, and

she grew more and more despondent, thinking miserably that she was failing in every way : unable to paint, convinced that she felt no return of the generous love which had taken her by the hand when she was verily 'friendless and an outcast;' conscious, with a feeling of guilty shame, that the chief interest of her life lay in those letters from Avice Wellfield, in which the girl poured out the whole history of her everyday life—all her hopes and fears, and her impressions of those around her—lamenting that there was one person, and one only, who seemed to be, as she said, 'above suspicion of being either morbid, or unhappy, or an impostor, or a victim,' and that one John Leyburn, over whose deficiencies of manner the fastidious young lady made constant moan.

Rudolf, during the whole winter, came very seldom, and stayed for a very short time— never longer than a couple of hours. Each time that she saw him, Sara felt more con-

strained, more guilty, knew less what to say,
or how to look, while his composure remained as imperturbable as ever.

And thus, after what had seemed an almost
endless winter, spring appeared.

CHAPTER VI.

T was May, and the whole land smiled under the consciousness of thraldom removed — of winter finally passed away. The old house was beautiful in the sunshine ; its grey walls set in a frame of trees, all bursting into the first exquisite spring foliage—of hyacinths and primroses, late daffodils and early wallflowers, all nodding their heads in the borders and on the flower-beds, and singing, most plainly to be heard by those who understand their language—

'Der Lenz ist gekommen,
Der Winter ist aus !'

Sara, after breakfast this sunshiny morning, threw a shawl around her shoulders, and went out into the garden to read a letter. As she paced about the sheltered, sunny south terrace, it was plain to see that she was at least restored to bodily health. There was almost all the splendid beauty of former days, yet somewhat paler and more refined. But the face was perceptibly changed. It was an older, sadder face—grander, but, as it looked now, far more sorrowful ; for there was not the inner contentment which gives the outward expression of peace. The eyes, which now and then were raised to survey the smiling spring landscape, were not filled with a deep, secure content. They were troubled, clouded, dissatisfied.

But presently she became absorbed in her letter. We may look over her shoulder and

read. It was one of those English letters,
whose advent Ellen did not love.

'My dear Sara,

'At last the day comes round on which
I may write to you. No doubt you were
perfectly right to say I must not write oftener
than once a fortnight, and I am sure, by doing
so, you saved yourself from being fearfully
bored; but it makes me wild with impatience
sometimes. It is such a comfort to feel as if
I were almost speaking to you—to feel that
in a few days you will be holding this that I
have written in your hand, and that for a
time at least you will be *obliged* to think of
me.

'Since I wrote, something very sad has
happened. Poor Mr. Bolton is dead. He
died last week, very suddenly, of heart disease.
You may imagine that it has been a fearful
blow to poor Nita, unhappy as she is already.
Even Jerome felt it, I think, or believed he

did. Mr. Bolton has always been so good to
him, and I defy anyone not to have respected
him. It made me very sad, too. I had got
so fond of him. Some of my happiest hours
were spent with him at Monk's Gate, helping
him with his Italian. He did so want to
finish his translation of the " Inferno," and
have it published. Nita liked me to go there.
Jerome always wanted her to stay in in the
evening, and I think she did not want her
father to see how sad she looked sometimes.
She is goodness itself, but oh ! so altered, so
subdued, and so sad ! I am sure she knows
by some means—though how, I can't imagine
—how dreadfully Jerome had deceived her
all the time she thought he loved her. At
least, I know that now she knows he does not
love her as she loves him, and as he *ought* to
love her. I know I am a fool sometimes. I
say such fearfully indiscreet things every now
and then. The other day, when Nita told me
that she hoped she would have her baby be-

fore next winter, I exclaimed, " Oh, Nita, how glad I am ! That will make it all right." She looked at me so strangely for a few minutes, and then burst into tears, and said, " Who knows ? who knows ? It is as God shall dispose it." I am glad she can think so. To me it seems very strangely disposed, but then, as you know, I never could say, " Thank God !" for the things that make everyone un-happy all round, and I don't believe they are providential at all. I believe they happen because people are wicked and selfish. But Nita is very good, though she never talks about it. I know she thinks people don't have troubles without deserving them, and she is under the impression that she must in some way deserve her troubles, though even she cannot say how.

' But I was telling you about Mr. Bolton's death. Everything seems very strange without him. Do you know, only the day before he died he gave me a lovely pearl

ring, which he said was to be in remembrance
of *my kindness to him!* How I did cry when
I thought of it. And poor Mr. Leyburn,
who, I am sure, never *will* learn when to
speak, and when to be silent, said that I
ought to be glad, and not sorry, to know that
I had been of any comfort to him. Now, *did*
he expect me to burst into a fit of delighted
laughter? But of course he means well.

'Mr. Bolton's death has made Nita, and I
suppose Jerome too, *very* rich, of course;
though I don't understand anything about the
circumstances of it.

'We are not so quiet here as I should have
thought we should be. All the people round
ask us out. Just before Mr. Bolton's death,
Jerome and I dined at Mrs. Latheby's. Nita,
of course, was invited too, but she will not go
out at present, and she would not let us stay
at home. So we went. There was Mrs.
Latheby, and her niece, Miss Paulina Bagot—
a Roman Catholic heiress, who is intended to

marry young Latheby. He was there too, with Father Somerville, who had come with him from Brentwood, Jerome and myself. We were the only heretics. Jerome sang, and I played, and young Mr. Latheby applauded wildly. Then Miss Bagot played, which she does exceedingly well. Mr. Somerville, as usual, made himself *very* agreeable. He really is one of the most delightful people I ever knew. I know you don't like him, but I call him charming. Both he and Mrs. Latheby are very polite to us. Mr. Somerville comes a great deal to the Abbey.

' Nita is like you—she dislikes him. At first when he came she used to sit with him and Jerome, and so did I ; but she felt so uncomfortable, she said, that now we always leave them in the library, and we go and sit in the drawing-room. Very often Mr. Leyburn is there too, for he does not like Father Somerville either, and has not the

good manners even to pretend to do so,
which annoys me very much. Sometimes
Mr. Bolton used to come, and then I used to
read to him about the savage tribes of South
America. We were reading the " Naturalist's
Voyage Round the World," which Mr.
Leyburn brought for us, about the only thing
in which his taste is unimpeachable. Of
course he listened with respect to that, but
all the other books he calls "travellers' tales."
He professes to go in for natural history
himself, or to be, as he calls it, "a bit of a
naturalist," and he was always interrupting
our reading, finding fault with the botany, or
the zoology, or the something ology of the
writers, which is a most exasperating habit.
It is so annoying, just as you are reading a
thrilling account of something, to be suddenly interrupted, " Incorrect! Where did
the fellow get his facts ? Not from accurate
personal observation, I'll wager."

' Miss Shuttleworth is just as amusing as

ever, but I don't think she has done any
thing *very* remarkable since I last wrote.

'Jerome still goes to business every day,
though I know Nita wants him to give it up.
I wonder that Nita never reproaches him!
But then he looks almost as miserable as she
does. It is a depressing household, dear
Sara, though I have nothing to complain of.
They let me do anything I like, and I
believe I might even come and see you if I
chose. But I have learnt a great many
things from the troubles I have seen since I
came here, and amongst others I have learnt
that I am of some comfort to Nita, therefore
I will not leave her.

'I must conclude. You will be tired of all
this. Do not be long in writing to me, if it
is only two sides of a sheet of paper.

'Ever your grateful

'A. W.'

Sara still walked to and fro, but in pro-

found and painful reverie. Her very soul
pitied her unhappy little successful rival.
She felt as if she would have liked nothing
better than to take Nita to her bosom and
soothe and comfort her, so intensely she felt
for the girl in her pain and desolation.
Could she by a word, even by some sacrifice
on her own part, have given Nita her husband's love, and wiped from her mind all
knowledge of his past transgressions, how
gladly she would have done it! for Sara, in
her solitude at *Mein Genügen,* had scaled
higher moral summits than she herself knew
—she thought she had not completely cast
away the old love, or the effects of it—she
did not realise that the substance of it had
been burnt away; what remained was a
shadow, a heap of ashes, retaining the shape
of that which was in reality consumed. It
was well that she saw the evil which remained, and not the good which was accomplished, else had she been in danger of suc-

cumbing to that 'palsy of self-satisfaction'
which has a trick of seizing upon and blight-
ing the finest natures.

But she knew that no word of hers could
give to Nita Wellfield her husband's love.
She felt, she had gathered from a hundred
unconscious little touches and admissions in
Avice's letters, that Jerome, like herself, was
not free. He loved her—Sara : yet sometimes she could weep, and wish it were not
so. Oftener she felt a half-contemptuous
satisfaction in the knowledge that he had not
been able to cast aside her power over him
with his promises to her. But oftener still
she had the feeling, which she instinctively
felt to be a far more dangerous one, of a
restless wonder what would happen if they
were to meet ; a wonder that sometimes grew
into something nearly akin to a longing.
Before this feeling she trembled, trying to
release herself from it, but it had a trick of
seizing her unawares, and mastering her.

And it was in such moments that she felt
what a slight division lay between her present
calm, monotonous existence, and the great
abyss opening under the feet of those who
yield to reckless impulses, or to what are
euphoniously called 'ungovernable passions.'

Such thoughts, and her meditations upon
Avice's letters, ran like a key-note through
her mental life at that time—tinctured all her
thoughts, her reading, her work; for since
she had begun to believe that she was never
to paint again, she had had resort to needle-
work, and was copying some curious old
Flemish lace, under the tutelage of a nun
from a neighbouring cloister. Under her
auspices, too, she had discovered some poor
in and around the town, and not only poor,
but ignorant; and she found some occupation
in helping and teaching them.

'That high-and-mighty Miss Ford turned
lace-maker and sister of charity—buried alive
in the dullest place in the world, and crying

her eyes out from pure *Langeweile*, because
she has displeased her husband, who is
jealous, and has shut her up there!'

Such was the account given by Frau Goldmark (who had a cousin in Lahnburg, with
whom she corresponded) to that very Fräu-
lein Waldschmidt who had been disabled
by scarlet fever from taking a share in the
tableaux vivants. When it is remembered
what language Frau Goldmark had formerly
used in speaking to Sara Ford of this very
young lady, it becomes almost impossible for
an impartial mind to acquit her entirely of a
spirit of time-serving.

Sara had been pacing about the terrace for
a long time, now and then reading over again
portions of Avice's letter, and anon lost in her
own mournful reflections. At last, raising her
eyes as she turned in her walk, she saw
Falkenberg's figure advancing towards her.
The first impulse that rushed across her mind
was to conceal the letter she held in her hand,

after which she found herself blushing hotly
at the idea of doing so, and thinking, with a
sudden prophetic fear, that it would be an
evil day—if ever it should dawn—on which
she could not meet his eyes. The uncomfortable sensation remained, however, that she
had been cherishing wrong thoughts —
thoughts best described by the hackneyed
term ' improper.'

She advanced to meet Falkenberg, and
held out her hand to him. She wished she
could have smiled and looked glad to see him,
in answer to the long and wistful look he gave
her ; but she felt more unhappy, more con-
strained in his presence than ever, and it was
with a look of profound gravity that she
greeted him.

' You did not expect to see me ?' said he.

' I always feel that you may or may not
come any day,' said Sara.

' You are better.   So your letters have
told me—so you look,' said he.

'Better—I am well in body,' she rejoined ;
and as she spoke, the same look of deep dejection returned—to her eyes the same cloud
as that which of late had constantly been
there.

'Not in mind ?' asked Rudolf, gently.

She shook her head.

'I wish I could say that I even felt as if I
were becoming better. Everything seems as
dark, or darker than it was before. Do you
see this letter ?'

She held it up, and her face was dark as she
spoke.

'Yes, of course.'

'It is from Avice Wellfield. I will tell you
the truth. It cannot be more bitter to you
than it is to me. These letters are the events
of my life, the only things I really care for.
I look forward to them with an eagerness I
cannot express, and when they have come, I
live upon the recollection of them. I cannot
find my place in this new life. I will not

deceive you,' she added, with a vehemence
almost passionate. 'I have not sunk so low
as to even wish to do that; but I feel degraded, humiliated, miserable, to think that I
cannot cast aside my weakness, that it dwells
with me. And as for returning to my old
pursuits—to my painting—to the joy I used
to have in even holding a brush in my hand
—I do not believe it will ever return to me
again. I believe it is destroyed. I have
heard of such things happening after a great
shock or a serious illness. I have had both;
why should it not be so with me?'

She spoke bitterly, though composedly,
and beat her hand with Avice's letter.

'And you do care for those letters?' he
asked.

'Yes—oh, if—do you object, Rudolf?
Would you like me to give over writing?'
she asked, with something like a ray of hope
dawning upon her face.

'Give it up—my dear child, I would not

deal such a blow to your poor little friend, or
offer such an insult to you, as even to hint
such a thing. To me, you are above
suspicion, Sara. If I heard you were
corresponding with Jerome Wellfield himself,
I should feel no uneasiness. I know you
and your pride and simplicity too well.'

' Ah, if only you had not been so chivalrous
and so mistaken as to marry me, Rudolf. I
fear it has been a terrible error on both sides.'

' Do you think so ? We had better give it
a little longer trial, I think, hadn't we ?' he
asked composedly, while he glanced rather
keenly at her face. ' Do you, perhaps, feel
tired of this place ? Would you like change
of scene or company ? Is there no one you
would like to have with you ? Miss Wellfield, for example ?'

' No. Avice has found a life at home. It
is astonishing how she develops, how quickly
she is growing into a woman, and a thoughtful
one. She finds that her sister-in-law needs

her presence greatly, and I gather from her letters, though she evidently has no idea of it herself, that she also will marry before long, and that happily.'

'Then you will not ask her to come and see you ?'

'No, thank you. I have thought about it, and I am sure that this is the best place for me. Solitude will not drive me mad. Let this be *Mein Genügen*—I will make it so for a time longer, if you will allow me. If I am to find peace anywhere, and a path through life, it will be here.'

'So be it. And since such is the decision you have come to, I may tell you the more freely that I have come to-day to say good-bye for a long time. I am going on a journey, and before I go I want to have a little talk with you on business, if you don't mind.'

'Going away!' uttered Sara, startled. Where ?'

' Oh, to wander about indefinitely—*auf eine*

Reise in's Blaue, as my own people would say. I am not going alone. A friend of mine, an artist, Rupert Schwermuth, goes with me, or rather, I offered to join him when I heard he was intending to travel and study. He means to go to Greece amongst other places, China, and Japan : he raves about Japanese art. I am going to rough it with him, by way of a change.'

Sara found she had absolutely nothing to answer to this. To object would, she felt, be worse than absurd ; to say she was glad would not be true, for with the knowledge that he was going so far away, came a sudden chill sense of prospective loneliness and deso-lation ; yet she must say something, she felt, and at last managed to stammer out :

' I think you do wisely. I hope you will enjoy your tour. But . . . . will you write to me ?'

' If you wish it,' he said. ' You seem tired ; take my arm. Do you mean just bulletins

from the successive stages of the journey,
or do you mean something more like
letters ?'

'I mean letters. I should like them exceedingly. I hope you will write.'

'I will write. And you—will you answer
my letters ?'

'What news can I possibly have to send
from here ?' said Sara, slowly.

'Tell me what you do every hour, from the
time you get up till the time you go to bed, if
you have no other news. It is not fair that
it should be all on one side. And if you are
anxious for letters, what shall I be, do you
suppose ?'

'I will write,' said Sara, in a rather low
tone.

'That is decided, then. Now, do you
mind coming into the house, for my time is
short, and I want to tell you something about
money matters.'

They went into the house, sat down at the

writing-table, and Herr Falkenberg from his breast-pocket drew forth a cheque-book.

'Do you see this?' he said. 'I have left directions with them at the bank to honour all your cheques, so long as you don't overdraw my private account,' he added, smiling. 'And this little book is to procure you the means of subsistence while I am away.'

'I will not be extravagant,' said Sara.

'No, don't, or I shall of course be exceedingly displeased. "Freely, but not extravagantly," is an excellent motto ; and you were born to devise and carry into execution schemes of economy.'

'Now you are laughing at me,' said Sara.

'Sometimes I cannot help it.'

'But why do you do it?' she asked, piqued.

'Heaven forbid that I should tell you why. You would never give me the chance of doing it again, and that would afflict me sorely.

Now I must go,' he added, looking at his watch, and rising.

'Go! No, you will stay for the Mittagessen, at least. You have never taken a meal in this house since I came into it—you, the master of it.'

'I wish I could stay. But you see, Rupert was to meet me——'

'Let him wait!' said Sara, with a heightened colour. 'Rudolf, I beg you to remain. You are not starting off to-day. Please do remain till afternoon.'

'*Wie du willst*,' he replied, using the *du* for the first time, as Sara instantly noticed.

'Thank you,' she answered; 'and here they are to say that lunch is ready. Shall we go to the dining-room?'

'I shall have to go directly afterwards, though,' said he, 'for poor Rupert will be cooling his heels at my house, wondering what has become of one who *never* fails to keep an appointment.'

'On which day do you think of setting off?' asked Sara, as they sat down to the table.

'To-morrow,' he replied.

'To-morrow! There is something remorse-less about to-morrow.'

The meal was not a long one. Sara was somewhat flushed and excited. She hardly knew what had prompted her to insist so strongly upon Rudolf's remaining, but she was glad she had done it.

He sat grave and composed as ever. Having made up his mind to the wrench of parting from her, he felt it rather increased his difficulty than otherwise when she displayed this sudden momentary gleam of—what was it?—a latent tenderness, or an amiability called forth by the fact that she was on the point of being rid of him for some months to come, and felt that the least she could do was graciously to 'speed the parting guest.'

Very soon after lunch was over he

said, very decidedly this time, that he must go.

'Must you, really? And—from what place will you first write to me?'

'Suppose we say from Trieste?'

'From Trieste—very well. I shall expect a letter from there.'

Both were speaking composedly, but Sara was on the verge of tears, and he was not unmoved, though he successfully concealed the fact.

'Good-bye, then,' he said.

There was a pause.

'I have a horror of saying good-bye,' said Sara at last, forcing herself to speak with an appearance of calm.

'Have you? It is one of the pains that attend the pleasures of life, I suppose.'

'Pleasures?'

'The pleasure of travelling, I mean. You can't go abroad without saying good-bye, unless you wish to be thought a monster.'

'Ah, you can joke about it. I cannot. And in a case like this, when you are going such a very long way off. Suppose—anything happened in which I wanted advice.'

'In that envelope you will find full directions, and the address of my confidential manager and head man—indeed he is more than that, and as he is a gentleman in every respect, you will be able to apply to him as you would to me.'

'Indeed I shall not, Rudolf!' she exclaimed, almost sharply.

Another pause.

'I am afraid my going will vex you; upset you. Would you like me to give it up?' he asked slowly.

'Oh no! no!' she answered hastily. 'Not for worlds! It was but a momentary folly. Let it pass! I hope you will have every kind of enjoyment on your journey.'

'Ah, Sara, I wish that momentary folly would recur oftener! But there! don't dis-

tress yourself. Remember this'—he clasped
both her hands, and looked with an earnestness that was almost solemnity into her eyes
—' *wherever* I may be, however I may be,
so that I am able to move at all, one word
from you will summon me back. *Here*, in
this house, or wheresoever you are, is *mein*
Genügen—my joy and my pleasure and contentment.'

Sara could not speak. As their eyes met,
she could not tell whether it was a great joy
or a great sorrow which that long, earnest
look foreboded. Falkenberg stooped and
kissed her forehead, said to her, ' *Lebewohl !*'
and was gone.

CHAPTER VII.

HE feelings were varied, the emotions complicated which, that
spring and summer, held sway in
the hearts of the household at Wellfield
Abbey.

At the time of Nita's marriage, Mr. Bolton
had retired to Monk's Gate, with his *Dante*,
and his books of voyages and travels; and
there Avice Wellfield had been of great
solace to him, as she had unconsciously
betrayed in her letters to Sara.

John Leyburn generously divided his
attentions between Monk's Gate and the

Abbey ; a plan which made little real difference in the amount of his company bestowed upon either place, for often the Abbey party would be at Monk's Gate, or Monk's Gate would go to the Abbey ; and thus they all met nearly as much as before.

At the Abbey, Nita was, as she always had been, the mistress. Jerome and Avice were the new elements. Jerome, probably by way of blunting disagreeable reflections, had taken in good earnest to business ; and if he did not care to reflect upon the means by which he had arrived at his present position, he had perhaps some comfort in the knowledge that *in* that state of life he was doing what approximated, at any rate, to his duty, so far as he knew how.

Mr. Bolton went seldomer to the office, and had begun to trust more power and responsibility into the hands of his son-in-law. He had privately told John that his health was

not all he could wish, but that he desired not
to alarm Nita, and he therefore confided to
him alone that his heart was wrong. He had
privately consulted a great doctor or two, and
they all said the same thing. He therefore
desired gradually to retire from the business.
Thus more and more work fell upon Jerome's
shoulders, and yet they were not overloaded.
He went eagerly and readily to work : in this
employment, which a year ago would have
been utterly distasteful to him, he found some
distraction ; for the atmosphere at home was
not altogether cheering. When a man has
acted in a base and cowardly manner, but yet
has sufficient moral sensitiveness left to desire
that his surroundings may think well of him,
it is a galling thing when one who is a portion
of those surroundings tacitly shows him that
she knows he has not been all that he ought
to have been—to her and to others ; and that,
judging, not by some superlative code of high
morality, but by the common hacked and

hewed standard of honesty and decency patronised by the ordinary, unremarkable man, that he has not even washed his hands in the common brown soap and water of this working-day world, let alone cleansing them in the finer and more subtle essences of chivalry.

For some months after their marriage Nita continued to worship her husband with a silent, intense passion of devotion which soothed and pleased him, even while he was uneasily conscious of a certain volcanic, sulphurous sort of atmosphere, while he had the idea that he was as it were standing on the edge of a crater—a position not without its discomforts. Nita never asked him any question as to that other love of which he had spoken to her; she appeared satisfied with his emphatic assurance that it was 'over, gone, passed away' entirely, and she rejoiced in what he did give her of tenderness and affection. He never knew what it was that

caused the change in her. He never asked,
for he dared not, or Nita might perhaps have
been able to tell him that one evening when
he was away, Father Somerville had called to
see him, and finding him out, had kindly
bestowed his society upon her for half
an hour. As it was, she never mentioned the interview except in the most
casual way, merely saying that Mr. Somerville had been disappointed to find Jerome
out. She did not mention that she had learnt
during that half hour her own true position
with regard to her husband, and his with
regard to her—that she had heard about it
without moving a muscle, and had sent
Father Somerville away entirely disappointed
of his hope to turn that position to his own
advantage. The holy father came and went
as before ; Mrs. Wellfield never condescended
to express any dislike to his visits. Jerome
knew nothing of this ; what he did know was
that Nita's whole manner and being had sus-

tained a nameless yet palpable change; she did not show him coldness, nor aversion, but there was a a wistful sadness, which gradually grew into a dejection—a quiet sorrow which at times tortured him.

It was very soon after she had learnt that she was to become a mother that this change became apparent in Nita. It was in vain that he lavished upon her every outward care and attention; that he watched her footsteps, and hung upon her looks, and attended her wherever she went. It was in vain that he would refuse invitations and tell her he did not care to go out until she could go out again too; in vain that he gratified, and even tried to anticipate her every wish : she faded and drooped before his eyes. And he dared not go beyond this outward form of devotion. He dared not ask the reason of the inward grief that consumed her, because he knew what the answer would be. He was perfectly satisfied that she knew something—how much

he knew not, and that again he dared not
ask—but something she knew of the deceit
he had practised towards her; that he had
taken her for his wife holding a lie in his
right hand. The position grew terrible,
even ghastly to him. Sometimes he wished
that she would reproach him; tell him what
she knew, ask him why he had treated her so
—then he could at least have promised that
since they were bound together, he would
never deceive her any more, but would
honestly devote his life to making her happy.
But Nita never did anything of the kind.
She was most gentle, and seemed to shrink
in every way from giving him pain. With
unstinting hand and ample generosity she
asserted his rights in everything, and showed
the most boundless confidence in him;
making a point, if anything of the slightest
importance were referred to her, of saying
that she knew nothing about it, they must
ask Mr. Wellfield. She never appeared to

shrink from being alone with him, though, when it happened that they were alone, she would sit for hours silent, unless he spoke. When he talked to her she always tried to keep up the conversation. But she was woefully and mournfully changed. Between her and Avice existed a great, if not a demonstrative friendship. Jerome was thankful for it, and that his wife and his sister had no unseemly disputes. The only times when Nita was really bright, or at all like her old self, were those occasions on which her father was with them. Then she would collect her energies (and Jerome painfully felt that her gaiety was the result of such a collecting of energy, and not spontaneous), and be even merry, and that so exactly in her old manner that her father never suspected anything wrong, and put down her somewhat wan face and languid movements to her physical condition.

'Are you happy, my child?' he asked one

afternoon, when he and she were strolling beside the river. This was very shortly before his death.

'Quite happy, papa,' she answered, and he concluded that the tears which filled her eyes as she looked up at him were tears of happiness.

'And Jerome is all he should be—eh?'

'You may see for yourself what Jerome is to me,' replied Nita, in a vibrating voice, and with a heightened colour. 'Surely no wife was ever treated with the attention that he gives to me!'

'Well, well, I was but joking,' he answered, with profound satisfaction. 'When I bought the Abbey, Nita, years ago, I often thought to myself that the Wellfields were a proud, extravagant race, and that their inheritance had passed away from them for ever, into hands that were honester than theirs, and better able to look after it. Then comes this youngster, and will have my daughter. It is strange—almost like a romance, I think, sometimes. It seems that a Wellfield is to have the old place again; it is not to be a Radical stronghold, as I had once fancied it would be. Better so, perhaps. At any rate, it was best that you should marry the man of your choice, be he rich or poor, Wellfield or Smith—and be happy with him. When I do go, I shall go in peace, knowing that you are settled in the home you love, with the man you love.'

' There never was anyone who had such a good father as I have. But he is very wicked when he says anything about " going," in peace or otherwise,' replied Nita, with something like her old smile.

After this they went into the house, and John came down to supper, for they still kept up the old hours, in every-day life, at least. Mr. Bolton also remained, and to all outward semblance a very happy, united family group was gathered there. Jerome offered to accompany his father-in-law to Monk's Gate, as he had wished to speak with him on a matter of business. The business was soon settled, and then, as they stood at the garden-door of Monk's Gate, Mr. Bolton suddenly said :

' Nita and I had a stroll by the river this afternoon. I was talking to her about you.'

' Yes ?' said Jerome, his heart giving a sudden throb as he wondered *what* they had talked about him.

' When you were married, I had some fears. Now I have none. I can see that my girl is happy. I wish you could have seen her face as she said to me, " You can see for yourself what Jerome is to me." Sometimes I think I shall not last very long——'

' God forbid that you should be right in your idea, sir.'

' Anyhow, Nita is all I have, and I thank you, Wellfield, for making her happy. It

gives to my old age all that it needs to make
it contented.'

He wrung Wellfield's hand, who answered,
in a voice of some emotion :

' My wife is an angel. I do not deserve
her.'

' Pooh ! "An angel not too bright and
good—" What is it ? I know I am quoting
it wrong, but it comes to the same thing.
Good-night, boy ! God bless you !'

Jerome, as he walked home, bit his lips,
and his heart seemed burnt up within him
with shame.

' Gad ! what a blackguard I feel when this
sort of thing happens !' he muttered, as he
went in.

Avice had gone to bed. John Leyburn
had departed. Nita was in her dressing-
room, where Jerome found her.

' You are tired ?' he asked, a new emotion
in his face and eyes, as he bent over
her.

'A little, dear. Nothing much. I suppose you are busy?'

'Yes. It is only a quarter-past ten. I am going to read for an hour. I have been— I mean your father has been speaking to me about you. He has been thanking me for making you *happy*. My God, Nita! How can I look at you and confess it! But some day'—he clasped her hand—'some day, you shall be happy—you shall, my wife.'

He dared not trust himself to say any more, but left her.

Nita sat still in the same position, not weeping—she did not very often weep now— but looking down at the wedding-ring on her hand, and wondering if that *some day* would ever come.

It was but a very few days after this that Mr. Bolton's death took place. Nita was very quiet, and apparently not much disturbed about it. She spoke about it to no one, except that when she first saw John

Leyburn after it, she thanked him for all he
had been to her father ; and she one day said
to Jerome that now the Abbey belonged to
him, she wished very much that he would
settle Monk's Gate upon Avice for her own,
unless he objected.

'And there is another thing,' she added ;
'I believe Avice and John are very fond of
one another, and I want you, if he proposes
for her, to give your consent.'

'Avice and John ! My dear child, you are
dreaming !'

'Oh no, I am not. I know all about it as
well as if they had told me ; and oh, Jerome,
don't come between them, please.'

'I think you are match-making a little ; but
if it should turn out so, I shall certainly not
oppose it, and I will see about Monk's Gate
being settled upon Avice at once.'

Nita thanked him, and the subject
dropped.

Mr. Bolton's will was much applauded by

all who heard of it, as being very just and
righteous—a pattern of a will. Needless to
go into details. The property was left to
Nita and her husband on trust, subject to
certain restrictions, for their lifetime, when
the bulk of it went to a prospective elder son,
proper provision being made for what other
children there might be, and for Nita, if she
were left a widow.

Having left behind him these right and
equitable provisions, Mr. Bolton was laid
away to his rest in Wellfield churchyard, and
allowed to sleep out his long sleep in peace.

After this the household at the Abbey
went on much as usual. Nita, though subdued, did not look utterly unhappy. Yet she
was a most unhappy wife, and Jerome knew it
well, and felt the unhappiness to be beyond
his power of curing. Nothing would restore
her happiness now, and nothing give her full
contentment, except the knowledge that he
loved her—perhaps not even that, if she knew

all of his conduct towards Sara—for Nita was tender-hearted. In the meantime, there was that unalterable fact—the past, the one thing that no power in the heavens above or in the earth beneath could make different, or cause to be as if it had not been.

Mr. Bolton was gone. John and Avice continued to bicker and squabble in a polite way, and were as much engrossed in one another as two really unselfish persons can be. Nita, as time progressed, kept more in the house, spent more hours on her sofa, with book and work, with Avice by her side, or Jerome, or alone with her dog Speedwell. She often sent them away, telling them she liked to be alone, and did not wish them to be tied to her. Jerome once uneasily inquired of Avice:

'Are you sure Nita really prefers to be left with her book ? What book is that she reads in so much ?'

For Nita always closed the book when he

approached, and laid it beside her in a manner which did not permit him to take it up.

' It is the *Imitatione Christi*, Jerome ; and I think she does like to be left with it,' said Avice, abruptly.

The one other intimate visitor beside John Leyburn, was Father Somerville. Nita saw very little of him. She now never offered the slightest remark upon his visits, almost ignoring them. Both Jerome and Avice imagined that her dislike to him had merged into a neutral feeling. Somerville himself, and he alone, was conscious how completely he was held at arm's length by the lady of the house, by the insignificant girl whom he had covertly sneered at many a time, even while he was advising Wellfield to marry her. He did not speak of it to anyone, but Nita's treatment of himself galled him, and it is to be feared that his bosom was not inhabited solely by that angelic mildness, that indifference to all slights and injuries which

Father Ravignac, at any rate, would have us believe animates the breast of every true Jesuit. Father Somerville had expected that Mrs. Wellfield would be unhappy; he had even taken active steps for making her unhappy, and he had expected that her unhappiness would cause her to take counsel with some one, perhaps with him, who so well knew how to invite confidence. But that unhappiness had had quite a different effect. It had transformed the 'insignificant girl' into a perfectly dignified, self-possessed woman— a very sad woman, certainly, but one who wore her crown of sorrow without cries or appeals—one whose grief was confessed, if at all, as between herself and her God—not to him, or to any like him. He was bitterly mortified, and while his keen insight told him the truth, he could not help admiring and wishing the more that he could gain any influence over her.

He had the more power over Jerome—a

power which he valued, though he would as
a matter of taste have preferred the other,
since there was assuredly more glory in being
able to influence a pure and exalted soul, than
one weakened by selfishness and enervated
by a feeling of self-contempt. He had not
failed to probe Jerome Wellfield's heart, as
opportunity was afforded. One day, in a fit of
almost intolerable remorse, when he had just
heard the news of Sara's having been at the
point of death, and of her marriage with
Falkenberg, and when, as it seemed to him,
his wife was fading away before his eyes,
consumed with her sorrow, Jerome had
confessed—it could be called nothing else.
The temptation of confiding in one whom he
felt to be so much stronger and more self-
sufficing—one whose hold on life and the
things of life was so much firmer than his
own, had proved too strong. Wellfield had
told him the whole story of his love for Sara
Ford—of his conduct towards her, and that,

when he dared to think of it, he loved her yet. For a short time it gave him relief, then Somerville let him know, by degrees, that he had fastened a chain about his wrists—that he was, to a certain extent, in his power; he hinted, in short, that Mrs. Wellfield might take umbrage at the story, if it were related to her. Wellfield cursed his own weakness for a time, and soon began to long inexpressibly for some change of scene, however fleeting. He had deteriorated—that goes without saying. Deterioration—mental and moral—is as natural, as inevitable a consequence of a series of actions such as his had lately been, as the sequence of the seasons, the rhythm of seedtime and harvest, of reaping and garnering is inevitable, as, to use the hackneyed scripture, to sow the wind and reap the whirlwind is inevitable.

But of course the deterioration had scarcely yet begun visibly to manifest itself. His wife's state had more influence with him than his own restless longings. His place was beside her—every voice of nature and of duty told him so, and he obeyed their mandate. The summer passed on. Nita did not expect her confinement until the end of October—and until that was over he must assuredly remain with her.

Things were, then, in this state at the beginning of October, when one of those things happened which do happen sometimes—little things in seeming, and which yet make grim sport with the greater things which seem of so much more importance.

A commercial house in Frankfort failed— a house with which Mr. Bolton's firm had always done a large amount of business. A meeting of creditors was called, at which it was highly desirable that principals should be present. Wellfield wished to remain at home and let it pass, but Avice having incautiously spoken about it, Nita insisted, with a determination that was almost vehement, that he should go. It was ascertained that he could easily go and return in a week, and as a telegram requesting his presence came to add to the pressure, he went one morning in the first half of the month.

CHAPTER VIII.

JEROME.

'There is nothing more galling than to receive pity where we would fain inspire love.'

THERE had been a long and stormy meeting of creditors—fierce disputes over the accounts which were brought forward, much vituperation, much gesticulation, and Jerome Wellfield had sat through it all, like a man in a dream, scarcely hearing a word.

He leaned back in his chair, his hands in his pockets and his face set, his eyes fixed frowningly upon the green leather top of the table at which he sat. Two sentences which

he had heard, earlier in the day, exchanged
between two gentlemen in the coffee-room of
his hotel, had banished all other subjects from
his mind.

'When is Falkenberg going to be back
from that immense *Reise in's Blaue* that he
undertook in May? and has he left his wife
alone all this time?'

'Oh, I fancy no one knows when he will be
back. His wife is at his place at Lahnburg.
She is very quiet, they say, and people think
they have had a quarrel. Don't know how
much of it is true, I am sure.'

He had heard every word of it. The two
speakers had sat at the next table to his as
he breakfasted that morning. Ever since,
heart and head alike had been in a tumult.
Not an hour's journey distant from him, and
alone! Of course he must not go to see her,
it would be the height of folly and presumption and wickedness; but could he not get one
glimpse of her, take one glance into her face

unseen by her ; have a view of her, perhaps, as she walked in her garden—or behold some outline of her form at the window. That would be enough. There would be nothing wrong in that; he could see her, and she would not see him ; having seen her, he could return home with a quieter heart.

The mention of her name, the knowledge of her proximity to him, had revealed, as such incidents do reveal, his own inmost soul to himself, and shrined there he found Sara Ford still, and knew not whether to rejoice that he yet loved her whose equal he had never seen, or whether to mourn that he could not cast that love aside, and content himself with the things that were his.

Thus he debated and debated within himself, endeavouring to find reasons why he should go to Lahnburg, while all the time, deep in his heart there was the full consciousness that he ought on no consideration to go near the place, that to do it would be an insult to Sara and to his own wife, and could bring nothing but misery to himself.

The meeting had been held at Frankfort in the forenoon, and was over by two o'clock. Jerome, when it was over, went into the hall of his hotel, and looking round, found what he had come for, though he had not even in his own mind confessed so much—a railway time-table fixed against the wall. He studied it, and saw that there were many trains on the Lahnburg line; one at five o'clock from Frankfort, arriving at Lahnburg at six. Three hours were before him in which to decide, and he said within himself :

' I will have some lunch, and think about it, but I don't think I shall go.'

Yet, when he had ordered some lunch and sat in the coffee-room waiting for it, he caught himself thinking what a long time it would be before the time came to set out for the station.

Should he go, or should he not ? He ate

and drank something, and strolled out of the hotel into the town, and passed by the people who wanted to show him the sights, and he thought he was trying to decide not to go. He repeated to himself all the arguments against going, and they were numerous and cogent. Then he caught himself wishing ardently that he had something to keep him in Frankfort—some engagement that would prevent his leaving the town that evening. Then he went back to the hotel and compared the clock there with his watch. A quarter before five. The station was close at hand—must he go, or must he stay? A man came up to him—one of the merchants who had been present at the meeting, and with whom he had a slight acquaintance, and said politely :

' Mr. Wellfield, if you are staying in the town, and have no other engagement to-night, will you do me the honour of dining at my house ? we are having some friends,

14—2

and I should be delighted to introduce you to my wife and daughters.'

' Thank you,' replied Wellfield, after a scarcely perceptible pause; 'you are very kind, and I should have been delighted, but I have an engagement out of town, and must go to the station now, if I am to catch my train.'

The die was cast, and he went quickly out of the hotel, and down the street to the station. Ten minutes later, he was in the train, on his way to Lahnburg.

When he arrived there it was dusk, as it is in October at six o'clock. He knew the place well, though he had not been of the party on that day of Sara Ford's first visit there. He knew the way, too, to Falkenberg's house, and quickly he walked there, and pushed open the gate, stood in the garden, and surveyed the old mansion. Behind one or two of the blinds he saw lights. Everything was very still in the dank, sad air of the

autumn evening. Not a sound came from the
house. The trees stood drooping and
motionless, saturated with the autumnal dew,
which is heavy and soaking and dank, not
lying lightly like a gossamer mist as that of
summer does. He could see the lights of
the town twinkling here and there, and a
faint hum came up from that direction ; but to
the right and straight before him there was
only a great veil of mist, hiding field and hill,
river and distance, alike.

He went up to the door, and rang the bell.
A man-servant opened the door, and Wellfield began :

'Is—' but his tongue refused to say
Falkenberg's name. 'Is the *gnädige Frau*
at home ?'

She was at home, he was told ; and Wellfield entered, and told the man his name.
The servant perhaps did not catch the
sound of the strange name, but seeing a
gentleman, composed and calm, asking for his

mistress, he concluded it was right, and opening the door of the salon, announced :

'A gentleman asks to see the gracious lady.'

Wellfield saw the lighted room, the figure seated, writing, at a table. A moment afterwards he was alone with her; she had risen and stood looking at him with a strange, alarmed, alien expression, which sent a dismal chill to his very heart. She did not speak. She stood looking at him, and, as he could not help seeing, with an expression of aversion, of shrinking distaste. Her hand grasped the back of the chair from which she had risen, as if for support.

His voice first broke the silence :

'Have I startled you, Sara ? Forgive me, but I——'

She drew a long sigh, as if then first realising that she was not in some strange dream.

'What—what brings you here ?' she asked in an almost inaudible voice.

'I was in Frankfort,' he said. 'By accident I heard your name, and heard that you were here and alone. I tried to fight against it, but the impulse was too strong. I felt as if I should repent it all my life if I did not see you once more, while I could.'

'You seem to forget that your visit must be very unwelcome to me; and that you had no right to come. Had I known of your intention I should have ordered my servant not to admit you. You must know that you are acting very wickedly.'

'*Wickedly!*' he repeated, scornfully and bitterly, 'of course I am wicked. Have I not been wicked all along? Do you suppose I do not know it?'

'I do not know, I am sure,' she repeated, in the same low, almost frightened voice, and with the same look of aversion in her eyes, and a sort of alarmed wonder, which expression galled him beyond what words can express; 'I do not know how wicked you

have been, but I think you forget yourself
strangely in thus forcing your presence upon
me. Will you go away, please, and leave
me? You can have nothing to say to me
that I can listen to, and I have nothing at all
—not one word—to say to you.'

'Not one? Have you no feeling for me,
Sara? Do you suppose that I am happy—
that I enjoy my life? Look at me! I look
happy, do I not?'

'I pity you from my soul!' she replied.
'And if my pity can be of the least use to
you, take it. I should indeed be inhuman if
I withheld it.'

She spoke very gently, never losing her
expression of pain and aversion. Wellfield
saw it; saw that she was bewildered, tortured by his presence. The scorn and the
withering contempt he had expected were
not there. What was there was far more
hopeless for him—much harder for him to
bear. He had had wild visions of falling at

her feet and forcing her to own that she, too, loved him as he loved her. Such a course was now out of the question. He felt degraded and humbled, and, worse than that —a fool—ridiculous and absurd.

'At least hear me when I tell you that I shall never cease to repent what I did in my madness. I shall never know happiness again, in feeling that I have destroyed yours, Sara.'

'You are quite mistaken,' she replied, sud-denly and clearly, as she stood up without support, folding her hands before her, and looking him full in the face. 'You have not destroyed my happiness; it is out of your power to do so. You turned it into bitter wretchedness for a time, I own. I am not superhuman. I loved you devotedly, and trusted you implicitly ; and when you betrayed me, I suffered as I hope few women do have to suffer. But you did not destroy my happi-ness, for that consists in loving and trying to do what is good and noble and honest, and you are none of them. But you cannot destroy those things, nor my joy in them, do what you will. Surely that is enough. Please leave me now, or I must ring the bell and ask them to show you out.'

' You mean to tell me that you will be happy married to Rudolf Falkenberg ? how do you account for that ?' he asked, unheeding her words, and advancing a step nearer to her, with eyes fixed upon her face, and breath coming and going eagerly.

Sara drew herself up, recoiling a step from before him. Then, looking at him with a glance devoid of the slightest feeling for him, she replied, in a deep, calm voice :

' Because he is all those things that you are not; he is good and noble and honest; he is faithful, and would be faithful unto death—because he saved me when you had almost killed me and quite driven me mad—and because he is my husband, and I love him.'

'You love——' he began, and stopped abruptly ; then, with a short, miserable laugh, said : 'After that I will go, certainly. And for the future I beg you will spare me your pity. I do not need it. Good-night.'

He turned on his heel and left the room. He did not know how he groped his way to the door and opened it, for he could see nothing. At last he found himself in the dank, soft, misty outside air again, just entering the market-square of Lahnburg, repeating her last words to himself over and over again, blankly, vacantly, and mechanically: ' Because he is my husband, and I love him.'

CHAPTER IX.

'Oh snows so pure, oh peaks so high !
I shall not reach you till I die !'
Songs of Two Worlds.

ELLFIELD found his way some-
how to the station, and waited for
the train to Frankfort, pacing
about the little asphalted platform with feelings of the most horrible shame and
humiliation—a longing to quit the place, to
lose the recollection of it—a sensation that he
belonged to a different world, a lower order
of creature than she did, and that to approach
her was folly, and must necessarily result in

disaster, in singed feathers and maimed pinions. Blended with this was a sudden yearning, stronger than he had ever felt before, to see once more the gentle eyes of the wife who, he knew, would never love any other than him, let his shortcomings or the nobility of the other be never so strongly contrasted. Truly, could his moral stature, his innermost *ich*, have been disrobed then and placed naked before the eyes of men, it must have presented but a sorry, grovelling kind of figure.

The slow, jog-trot train came rumbling in, and bore him in leisurely fashion past all the little stations, till at last, long after half-past eight, they arrived at Frankfort.

He trailed his steps slowly up the street to the hotel. What he had just gone through mentally—the moral scourging he had just sustained, had exhausted him more than the hardest day of physical exertion could have done. He felt used up—*todtmüde*, as he dragged himself up the steps into the dazzling light of the hall, filled with piles of luggage and groups of visitors—men smoking, girls flirting with them, parties of people taking their coffee, an incessant passing to and fro, and cheerful bustle.

It seemed that there was to be no pause, no reprieve in the sequence of his calamities just then. A waiter came up to him, and asked if he were the person to whom '*dieses telegram*' was addressed.

Mechanically he took it; his apprehension dulied with the moral castigation from which he was freshly come, and opened it, dully wondering from whom it came, and what in the world it was about.

'*John Leyburn,*   *To Jerome Wellfield, Esq.,*
      Wellfield.   — *Hotel, Frankfort-am-Main.*

'Your wife has a son. She is very ill. Return at once, or you may be too late.'

For the first moment this seemed the one

drop too much. With a kind of faint groan, he dropped into a chair that stood hard by, and propped his throbbing head upon his hands, feeling as if to move another step would be impossible.

But this was but for a moment. He raised his head at last, and saw that one person had been compassionate enough to come forward, and speak to him—a stout, comely English matron, who, bravely overcoming her insular reserve, said :

' I fear you are ill. Is there nothing we can do for you ?'

He raised so haggard a face, such wretched eyes towards her, that she half-started ; but Jerome, touched inexpressibly by the one drop of sympathy of this motherly-looking woman, answered brokenly :

' I am not ill, madam, I thank you. I— my wife—you may see——'

He put the paper into her hand, and went upstairs to put up his things, and hasten to the night train for Brussels and Calais, which he knew left in about half an hour's time. When he came down again, and had paid his bill, and was going out into the night with his wretchedness, the same kind-looking matron stepped up to him, and said, all her stiffness melted away :

' I hope you will find your wife better, and not worse, when you get home. I can feel for you, and I shall think of you, for I have daughters of my own.'

' Thank you for your goodness—you are very kind,' he said quickly, his voice breaking, as he hurried away.

' Poor young fellow ! I wonder if his wife will get better,' said the prosperous-looking matron to her husband.

' Pooh, my dear ! A perfect stranger ! The thing is sure to be in the *Times* if she does die. That "poor young fellow" must be young Wellfield of Wellfield. I wonder how he came to be here.'

' He has a great trouble of some kind, and I hope his poor wife will not die,' repeated the lady.

*   *   *   *   *

The kindly words of the strange lady put a momentary warmth into his heart, and he thought of them more than once on his journey home.

We all know what a journey from such a place to London is. Jerome, inquiring on the way, found that with the best will in the world he could not be in Manchester before nine o'clock the following night, and from Manchester how was he to get to that out-of-the-world place Wellfield? He dared not stop to think of it, but made his way onwards as fast as he could. The twenty-four hours of travelling and waiting, and waiting and travelling, seemed an eternity. He knew how they must all be waiting for him, and Nita—he stopped that thought instantly

—it never got so far as the wonder whether she were dead or alive.

Manchester at last—after time, on a clear moonlight night. Into a hansom, with urgent demands for speed, from the London Road Station, down the long length of noisy Piccadilly and Market Street, up the hill to the Victoria Station. He breathlessly asked the porter who strolled up to him, ' The train for Wellfield—how long ?'

' Last train left twenty minutes ago, sir— the slow one—doesn't get in till eleven.'

' I *must* be there to-night,' he repeated, mechanically.

' There's an express to Bolton, sir, in five minutes. If you took that, you might perhaps have a special on from there.'

This was the only plan, and he took it. He was in Bolton in half an hour. A few inquiries there. Yes—they would send him on with a special if he liked, but not for an hour. The line was blocked, and it could not be done before then.

A sudden thought struck Jerome. One of his horses had been sent to Bolton two days before he left, for a certain dealer to dispose of : he knew it must still be there, for he had left orders that nothing was to be concluded about it till his return. The man's place was close to the station, and it was but ten o'clock. It was a twenty miles' ride to Well-field, but with a swift horse he might be there sooner than by waiting an hour for a special train.

How it was settled he knew not. His white intent face, and something of a silent urgency in his whole manner, caused the men to hasten their work. In little more than ten minutes he rode out of the town along the great north-eastern road.

It was a moonlight night, and bitter cold— a contrast to that of twenty-four hours ago. He settled himself into his saddle, set his

teeth, and tried to think it was a short way.
He never confessed the feeling to himself, but
he had little hope—his feeling was, not that
he hastened to give Nita the comfort of his
presence as soon as possible, but that he rode
a race to speak to her and hear her speak to
him before she died.

The horse was fresh, was ready, and will-
ing for the work ; he shook his head,
stretched his long legs and lean flanks, and
' his thundering hoofs consumed the ground.'
Bending his head before the bitter air,
Jerome gave him rein, and they flew quickly
past village and farm and town, through one
great dingy mass of square buildings and tall
chimneys after another ; through streets
dazzling with lights, and flaring gin-palace
windows, into a long stretch of quiet country,
with the moon shining serenely on the silent
fields.

It seemed an eternity till he came to Burnham, the last great town before Wellfield,

and some six miles away from it. Outside
the town, beside a brook, he paused to water
his horse ; then, with a word of encourage-
ment, and a pat on the neck, the good beast
resumed its long, swinging stride, and there
at last, in the moonlight, he sees the first
home landmark, the great shape of Penhull,
grey and ghast in the moonbeams. Nearer
and nearer to that well-known shape, till he
saw the long wooded ridge on which Brentwood stands, and then down a hill, betwixt
thick woods ; there stands the old white
church at the end of the street, here he is on
the stones of Wellfield village—up its whole
length in a moment's space, in at the Abbey
gate—his horse's hoofs sound hollow on the
turf of the river walk. The gate stands open ;
his eye scans the windows. That was Nita's
room, and a light shone behind the blind.

He flung himself off his horse, and almost
staggered into the house. The drawing-room
door stood wide open, and as he entered a

man came out; he looked desperately into
the face of Nita's old friend.

'Leyburn—my wife—is—is she——'

'Yes, she is living still,' said John, putting
his arm within his, and leading him to the
foot of the stairs. 'In her own room,' added
Leyburn. 'Miss Shuttleworth and your
sister are——'

'Yes—thanks!' he answered, running up
the stairs and finding himself at last in the
subdued light of Nita's room, hearing Avice's
voice exclaim :

'Oh, Jerome ! Thank God !'

He neither saw nor heeded anyone, but
strode to Nita's side, and knelt by her bed,
controlling himself with a great effort.

'Is it you, Jerome ?' said a feeble changed
voice. Avice and Miss Shuttleworth had
left them, the latter sobbing uncontrollably.

'Don't speak, Nita, my darling ! I am
here, I shall never leave you till you are well
again !' he murmured.

' I must speak, Jerome. I want to say—
you will love my baby—oh !' She began to
weep pitifully.

' Hush, hush !' he implored her. ' Nita,
hush ! Let me love *you*, my child.'

' And you will not let him forget that *I* was
his mother, and should have loved him dearly
if I had stayed with him,' she went on, in a
voice ever fainter and fainter.

' You shall teach him yourself, my wife.
Ah, Nita, you must not leave me! God
knows how I need you and your love and
your forgiveness!'

' Jerome,' with a sudden flicker of life and
strength, 'do you love me a little ?'

' As God is above us, Nita, I love you
dearly,' he answered ; and he spoke what was
the truth at the moment, at least.

' I am glad that I was able to speak to you,
she said. ' But if——'

These were the last words. When,
alarmed by the long silence, Avice and Miss

Shuttleworth entered the room, they found Wellfield kneeling still beside his dead wife, holding her cold hands to his breast, and motionless almost as herself.

CHAPTER X.

A FEW days later, Nita was laid to her rest in the churchyard at Wellfield, beside the father who had loved her so well, hard by the paved footpath leading to the church-door. Many feet would daily pass beside her grave: lovers walked through the churchyard; the old people strolled there to sit on the bench by the porch at sunset; the feet of those who were full of life and business hastened constantly to and fro; for the gates were always open, and the churchyard path was a much-used thoroughfare.

When it was all over, Avice put her hand through her brother's arm, and turned to the two other persons who had come with them as mourners—John Leyburn and Father Somerville.

'I think we will go home alone, if you do not mind,' she said, offering her hand first to one, and then to the other of them.

Wellfield did not speak; his gaze was blank, and he scarcely knew or saw who was there, or what had passed.

'I will come this evening and ask after you,' said John; 'and you can see me if you choose.'

With which, and with a mute inclination of the head to the others, he went away to his home. A new love, fresh and strong, had sprung up in his heart. But he had loved Nita well, too, with faithful, brotherly love, and his heart was heavy. Her going made a great blank space in his life.

Somerville turned to Avice, and said in a low voice :

'If it gets too much for you, Miss Well-field '—he glanced significantly at Jerome— 'send for me, and I will come instantly.'

With which he, too, turned and left them.

Slowly they walked from the churchyard, in at the Abbey gate, up the river walk, and towards the house.

It was a soft, mild October noontide. The sun shone with mellow, tempered warmth ; the hues were varied of the fading leaves and the autumn flowers ; birds chirped here and there, and the river rushed, as the two figures, black, and, as it seemed, incongruous, paced slowly up the walk. As they entered the house, Avice said pleadingly :

'Jerome, won't you go and see Nita's baby ? He is such a lovely child. I am sure it would make you less grieved.

'No, no ! not yet, at any rate.'

'Do you know, that when he was born we thought he would die? Father Somerville called to ask about you—he did not know you were away—just as they were about to send for the vicar to baptise him; and he offered to do it, so they let him, for fear it should be too late if they waited—for his poor little life seemed to hang by a thread.'

'Why do you say *they?*' asked her brother.

'Simply because to me it seemed absurd—as if it made any difference to the poor little darling whether he was baptised or not! Will you not go and see him, Jerome?'

'Perhaps—presently. So *Somerville* baptised him!' he said dreamily; and then added:

'I am going upstairs to her sitting-room.'

'Don't stay there too long, Jerome. It makes me so unhappy to think of you.'

'You must not mind me,' was all he said, as he slowly took his way upstairs.

Passing the rooms which had been set apart

as nurseries, he heard a child's feeble cry, and
started, shuddered, and hastened his steps till
he came to what had of late been Nita's
favourite room—a little boudoir opening from
her bedroom.   There was a dimness, subdued and faint.   He stood on the threshold,
looking round, and by degrees began to
distinguish things more clearly.   They had
not drawn up the blinds here since Nita had
last been in the room, the evening before she
was taken ill.   Everything was as she had
left it.   There was the couch on which she
had spent so many weary hours, and the little
table beside it, on which lay one or two
books, and her writing-case, and a work-
basket.   Another book had fallen upon the
floor, and something lay beside it, in which
Jerome, looking intently, recognised Nita's
great dog, Speedwell, stretched upon the
ground beside the couch, waiting, no doubt,
for her return, and watching the book which
had fallen ; it was the book she had read in

so much of late—her little 'Imitation of Christ.'

The old dog looked up, with a wistful expression, whined a little, and waved his tail to and fro, as Jerome looked at him. With an inarticulate sound, which ended in a heavy sob, the young man dropped upon one end of the couch, covering his face with one hand, while the other hung down, and the dog licked it, and sat up, and whined again, asking where she was.

His anguish at this moment amounted to torture, as he realised how completely everything had come to an end. Here, as he sat alone, with his own miserable thoughts—here and in this moment his wages were paid to him ; measure for measure—no more and no less ; wages which could not be refused, could not be transferred, must be accepted and counted over, and tasted to the bitter end.

Let the future hold what it might, this

hour could never be wiped out. In his then state of mind, he could not see any future at all ; he could see nothing but the past—could realise nothing except that he had played a dishonest game, and had lost ; and that at every turn in his mental path he was confronted by an 'if.' 'If I had done this !' 'If I had told her that !'

He did not know how long he remained in Nita's room, feeling the tokens of her recent presence on every side like whips of fire, but when he left the room and went out of the house, it was dusk, and he mechanically took his way towards a field-path by the river, along which one could wander for two or three miles uninterrupted by gate or stile, or barrier of any description. It was lonely and beautiful ; it had been one of Nita's favourite haunts.

The path led sometimes through a kind of lane, with a high hedge on either side, and again through broad, level fields beside the

river, towards Brentwood, with glorious
views of hill and wood on every side.

Between those hedges and through those
fields Wellfield wandered as one distraught
—not with any outward appearance of dis-
order, but with inwardly such an agony of
remorse and self-reproach as was rapidly
gaining the ascendency over his judgment
and reason. Long fasting, and watching
beside that cold mask which had been all
that remained of Nita's countenance, and
upon whose placid features he had thought
to detect a fixed and marble reproach, silent
but terrible, and which haunted him cease-
lessly—all this had combined to raise him
into a wild, excited frame of mind, in which
he was scarce master of his impulses or
actions. As he watched, in the rapidly-
gathering dusk, the deep and swiftly-running
river, the desire presented itself again and
again to quench therein this unabating torture
of mind : each time the temptation came more

insidiously, and the plausible excuse incessantly recurred, that he had proved himself unfit to manage his own affairs, and that those who were left behind would much better manage those of his child—his child whom he had not yet been able to look upon.

It went so far that at last he stood beside the river, and looked and looked, until to his morbid perceptions it seemed to shape its murmurs into words that invited him to come. Deep down in his nature he was profoundly superstitious. There was an old record of a Wellfield who had been unhappy, and had destroyed himself in this very river. Jerome thought in his madness, 'Well, wherever he is, I may go too, I suppose. There can be nothing in the future—on the other side, as bad as this. . . I believe all I have gone through has been sent to show me that I have no right to remain here any longer . . . besides, a life for a life! I have taken Nita's, and . . .'

He stood on the very edge of the stream towards which he had unconsciously drawn, and was looking down into it as it hurried past, with a vague, fascinated gaze. Would it ever have come to the point of throwing himself in? Probably not. Suicides are not such as he. His remorse doubtless was horrible. But if he *had* taken that cold plunge, it would have been, not from a sense that he was too unworthy a wretch to live, but because life was so intensely uncomfortable— to *him*. Be that as it may, he stood on the brink, in a dreamy ecstasy—a luxury, as it were, of grief and self-reproach, interspersed with vague wonder why women would fall in love with him, when :

'You walk late beside the river, Wellfield,' said Somerville's voice, while at the same moment the priest laid his slender, fragile-looking, yet muscular fingers upon his arm.

' Ah!' breathed Wellfield, with a kind of prolonged sigh; and then, looking up, he could see, even through the gathering darkness, the calm, clear, commanding eyes which were fixed upon his face. The stronger nature subdued him—subdued everything about him : his anguish of remorse ; his poignant grief; his wild desire to bring his misery to an end in some way or other, but to put it to an end. He felt that Somerville had read his half-formed wish, nor did the latter hesitate to avow it.

' You had no good purpose in your mind ?' he said, composedly.

For all answer, Wellfield gave a half-groan, and propped himself up against an ancient, gnarled crab-tree which overhung the stream. Then, after a pause, he said :

' I had no purpose at all, except to end my wretchedness. I tell you I cannot live through much more of this. Why did you come in my way ?'

'Because another lot is appointed to you
than to make an end of yourself in that river,'
was the reply; 'and I—I recognise it distinctly—was sent to tell you of that different
lot.'

'Then give me peace—give me ease from
these torments that I am enduring,' said
Wellfield, fiercely, his sombre eyes, clouded
over with his anguish, flashing suddenly.
'You it was who first put the cursed idea
into my head of marrying that girl; you told
me then, when I hesitated, that if I belonged
to you—you could make it all smooth and
right for me. Make it right now—now that
I have murdered her and got her money.'

'Yes, I will do so,' was the rejoinder, in a
tone of such perfect assurance, such calm conviction, that his hearer felt it strike something
like conviction to his heart. 'You are in a
labyrinth, but I can guide you out of it, for I
have the clue. Yield yourself only to my
guidance. That is all I demand. And for me

to guide you, I must know *all*, unreservedly
—every secret of your heart, every thought
that distracts you. Then I can help you.'

Who shall deny the healing virtue of confession now and then? The temptation to
confess now was irresistible to Jerome; to
Somerville it suddenly gave the power he so
ardently desired; suddenly, and far more
easily than he had expected. It was not the
first case, by many, of remorse gone mad,
which he had had to deal with. A dullard,
an unsympathetic nature might have driven
the patient to worse lengths. Somerville
was neither the one nor the other, and by
this time he thoroughly understood the nature
he had to deal with—the hot southern im-
petuousness which raged and rebelled under
misfortune, which met grief as a hated foe, to
be wrestled with—not as a fact inseparable
from life itself, to be accepted; the half-
hysterical remorse, the stinging, intolerable
sense of humiliation and degradation which

so tortured the man who loved to see things smooth, and to find circumstances bland. Somerville's hand was at once light and firm. Walking with Wellfield to the Abbey, he heard out the whole miserable story; the confession of all that had happened from the time Jerome had left Wellfield for Frankfort, up to this very day, when he had gone into Nita's room and found her old dog watching beside her couch.

It was an opportunity which the priest did not fail to turn in a masterly manner to the very best advantage. Already he saw the Abbey and its wealth once more in the hands of firm adherents of the Roman Catholic Church—of the Society of Jesus. Had not the child been, by his own hand, baptised into that Church? He distracted Jerome's mind from its purely emotional pain, by reminding him that Nita and her father had left things behind them—the one land and money, the other a life—for the disposal of which things he alone was now answerable.

He found Wellfield only too ready to own that he wanted guidance, only too eager to clasp the first helping hand extended to him. Somerville remained all night at the Abbey, with every hour binding his silken chain more firmly and more intricately around his —penitent. He sent word to the Superior at Brentwood on what mission he was engaged, and during the long vigil he kept with the broken man, he succeeded in the most vital part of the work which he had set himself. He convinced Wellfield that he was indispensable to his peace of mind, and he promised not to desert him.

In the morning, before leaving for Brentwood, after promising that he would return again, Somerville, passing through the drawing-room, found Avice standing there, with the motherless baby in her arms. She held it tenderly, with a motherly, protecting gesture, and looked down with love and pity into its face. He paused, smiling, and said :

' I have forgotten to ask how your charge goes on, Miss Wellfield ?'

' Both nurse and the doctor say he is going to thrive, father. Look into his dear little face—he looks rosy and healthy. Poor little darling, how I love him! and how I wish Jerome would take to him !'

' I will do what I can to persuade him when I call again. At present he is utterly worn out with grief and watching.'

' Yes,' said Avice, tears dimming her violet eyes. ' Do you know, I did not think Jerome cared so much for my sister as it seems he does. I have done him an injustice.'

' One naturally cares more or less for the person who is of most importance to one,' replied Somerville, with a sweet and polished smile. He looked again at the child, whose dark eyes dwelt unconsciously and with the vague, meaningless gaze of infancy upon his face, and bending over it, he blessed it, slow and solemnly. ' Since I baptised him, I may do that ?' he said.

' Surely !' replied Avice ; and added, with a musing look, ' Oh, if Nita could have but lived to see him like this, I think mere love would have given her courage to fight her way back to life again, and she would have struggled through.'

' It may be so,' replied Somerville, wishing her good-morning, and wondering within himself, as he went away, how long it would be —whether he should be still living, and still teaching, when that baby should be a student at Brentwood. ' For that he will be,' he said within himself. ' What strides I have made in this affair ! and how truly providential that the mother died at that precise time ! Had she lived, we should never have had the child . . . . and if he marries again, we must see that the woman is a Catholic.'

CHAPTER XI.

HEN Wellfield left her, Sara sat down, trembling and unnerved. But that sensation was not of long duration. Soon she recovered, and was astonished at the sudden lightsomeness of heart which she felt. It was as if some thunder-cloud had burst, had discharged its flood of storm-rain, and dispersed, leaving a sky behind of a blue etherealised and idealised. It was not the effect she would have expected—the very reverse; it gladdened her as unexpected joy does gladden. She did not mention, even to Ellen, the visitor

she had had. She had a plan in her mind,
which came there spontaneously ; she found it
there ; it gladdened her, thrilled her, filled her
eyes with happy tears. She would make it
the pretext for telling Rudolf that she loved
him ; she would so tell the incident of Jerome's
unlucky and reckless visit to her, that no
doubt should remain in her husband's mind
as to what she meant, for as to speaking
out the words to him which she had said
with such boldness and composure to Wellfield—the very idea of it was impossible.

Ellen, as she helped her mistress to undress,
wondered greatly what could cause the
frequent smile, and the brightened eyes
which she instantly noted.

The next morning was a clear, glorious
autumnal one; a white mist enveloped the
valley, and covered the river and the fields
which bordered it, and the long rows of
poplars between which it flowed, while the
tops of the hills stood out, clear and distinct,

bathed in a flood of golden sunshine, and the
sky above was like a sapphire for clearness
and depth of hue.

Sara drank in deep draughts of the sweet,
bracing air, and as she looked around, her
heart swelled within her, and an impulse
which for months had slumbered—had been
as though it had never inspired her, animated
her once more—the desire, namely, to take
her brush in her hand, and picture that scene
as once she would have had great joy in
doing. But after first arriving at *Mein
Genügen* she had had such an impulse often,
and nothing had come of it; when she had
tried to reduce it to action, she had been so
disheartened with the dulness, the utter
absence of life, of the old strength and craft,
that it was now long since she had renewed
the attempt. This morning, though the
impulse was at first strong within her, she
shook her head, and decided not to make an
attempt which must end in disappointment.

She opened her book, and tried to be interested in that.

Soon the effort succeeded. It was an Italian history, which she had found amongst Falkenberg's books, and the page at which she opened it pictured that scene in which *il rè galantuomo*, contrary to the advice of his great minister, and other wise and potent counsellors, had insisted on preserving in the speech from the throne which he was to utter on opening parliament, an allusion to the sufferings of his people, and his own sensibility to them. That 'cry of anguish'—that *grido di dolore* of which the King spoke, has now become historical. Sara did not remember even to have read of it before, or, if she had, she had passed it by, and forgotten it. What drew her attention to it on this occasion was a mark in pencil beside the sentence, and at the foot of the page, on the margin, the words, in her husband's handwriting:

'Surely a fine subject for a picture, treated either allegorically or literally.—R. F.'

Sara's hands, with the book in them, sank gradually, and she raised her face, full of musing and reflection, towards the clear hill-tops, whose bases and all beneath were swathed in mist.

'It *would* make a grand picture,' she mused, 'for all who knew the allusion. *Il grido di dolore* . . . When Victor Emmanuel spoke those words they were prophetic of the release of his people—of their salvation. There spoke the deliverer. The scene should not be all a cry of anguish; there should be a tone of hope as well. It would be best treated allegorically, I believe. I suppose, if I treated it as I should wish, I should be called narrow and feminine in my idea. No doubt I should make it personal —turn Italy into a human being—bring my own experience to bear upon it—what has my language been of late but a *grido di dolore;* more shame for me, no doubt! I wonder how *he* thought of its being represented. I wish I knew. Surely any real representation of the thing should show not only the lower creature crying aloud in its agony, but the strong spirit which has heard its cry and will raise it up.'

Again she looked across towards the hills. The mist had almost all cleared away. The river was now perceptible, winding in silver links towards Coblenz; the poplars and the fields, the red-roofed villages and the peaceful homesteads, all came into view. Upon her spirit, too, fell a peace which it was long since she had experienced. She went into the house, and found that the post had come in, and that breakfast awaited her. There was one letter for her, and that was from Falkenberg. Throwing off her hat and shawl, she eagerly opened and read it. It was from Rio—so far had they progressed in

their wanderings—and it gave her a graphic
account of their recent expeditions, of the
glowing beauty of the Brazilian scenery, and
of the odd, eccentric habits of his companion.

' I think you would like him, though. He
has real original genius beneath all his
whimsicalities, and some of his sketches are
masterly.' Then he went on to say that
their movements were undecided ; they did
not know whether to make a further journey
or to return to Europe.

He made many inquiries after her health,
her pursuits, her happiness, and begged her
to write very soon. ' You cannot tell with
what eagerness I look for your letters. You
will not quarrel with me for saying this, since
I am such a long way off. Sometimes the
longing to see your face is so intense that I
feel as if I must start up, and be off then and
there—*auf der stelle ;* but do not be dismayed.
The aberration, when it comes, is only tem-

porary. You need not dread my bursting in upon you suddenly, without preparation ; that is, if you will keep me pacified by some more letters like your last one.'

She finished it breathlessly, and, as if by a sudden, irresistible impulse, pressed the paper again and again to her lips, with passionate earnestness.

'Oh !' she murmured to herself, ' would that you were here ! Will anything step between us ? anything come to keep you and me apart *now* ? I cannot think that the end of this story will be all that it should be. And now I shall tremble always, till I see you —and—perhaps even then. Who knows ?'

Later in the forenoon, she felt again irresistibly impelled to try once more if her old craft had not come back to her. She took a canvas, and her palette and brushes, and tried to sketch in some representation of the scene which had haunted her ever since she had seen the pencilled words at the foot of

the page. Again she opened the book, and
again read the words : ' I am not insensible to
the cry of anguish—*il grido di dolore*—which
arises from my faithful people in all parts of
my kingdom.' As she drew, her heart beat
ever faster and faster. It was a man's figure
that she outlined ; the figure of a king, it was
intended for—of one who, by nature and by
circumstance, was a ruler. Her crayon moved
more slowly as she tried to infuse into this
figure some of the royalty of bearing and look
with which, in her own mind, she invested
the form of this ' deliverer.' When, after a
couple of hours' diligent drawing, the outline
stood out clearly before her, she looked at it,
and saw that it was good ; it *was* kingly,
dignified ; majestic and benevolent too. She
had not failed. She was not to be robbed for
ever of her old power. Her art had been
restored to her.

That, she felt, was enough for one day.
She had not been aware with what intense

eagerness she had longed that she might prevail—that life and skill might be restored to
her hand, until, when she at last saw that 'it
was so,' she broke down, and burst into a
passion of tears—but tears which, if stormy
at first, soothed and healed in the falling.

It was evening of the same day. Sara sat
down in the quaint old salon, in the flickering
firelight. There was an open English grate in
which pine-logs were burnt, for the appearance
of comfort; and there was likewise a porcelain
stove to produce the reality of it. She had
sent away the servant who came with lights,
saying she would ring when she wanted them;
and now, with her cheek propped on her hand,
she sat and gazed into the fire—into the red
map of the land of dreams. It was indeed a
vague, aimless dream in which she was lost;
and yet there was an undercurrent of passion
about it, a solid basis to the vision. That
letter from Rio, which she had had that morning, which lay open in her hands now, which

she had just been reading, and which had
wafted her on its thin pages away from this
place altogether. She pictured to herself tro-
pical climes and South American forests.
Could he be perhaps wandering with his
friend in the solemn, desolate splendour
and luxuriance of such a forest, even now?
At least, wherever he was, he was hundreds of leagues away from her. She had
visions of stately vessels borne onwards by
soft south-western gales—gentle gales. So,
equally, she could see, in the map that was
constantly changing its boundaries by a
process of crumbling, visions of fair and busy
cities—foreign cities, full of pleasure and
gaiety, most beautiful to behold, but all a very
long way off—hundreds, yea, thousands of
miles away.

The great distance, the feeling that if
anyone asked her, ' Where is he now?' she
could only answer, ' I know not!' weighed
her down with an unspeakable despondency.

Then, like a flash of fire across this chill mood
of resignation, darted a longing, intense and
uncontrollable, to have him there, at that very
moment. Oh, if he would but come! If he
would but come! Could he not understand
the meaning her last letters had tried to convey? Could he not read, 'I love you,'
between the lines? This intense, concen-
trated longing for the bodily presence of
some deeply-loved personality is a painful
thing when one longs and goes on longing
in spite of the secure knowledge that no
amount of longing will bring that person to
one. Thus it was with her. She covered
her face with her hands presently, and her
heart throbbed. Did he in this moment
experience half of the same feeling? If she
could have thought it, she would have felt
almost satisfied. But how could he? She
raised her head, and looked round the room
—her favourite, because it was into it that he
had led her and Countess Carla, on that far

back, happy red-letter day whose full worth
and meaning she had only within the last
weeks began really to realise.

'Could not a miracle happen ?' she thought ;
'could not he have followed quickly on the
footsteps of his letter, and—but heaven forgive my presumption ! Why should such
notice be taken of *me*?'

Even as she thought it, a cloud seemed to
come before her eyes; her very breath to
stop. Yet she was rising from her chair,
advancing to meet the ghost—to prove the
miracle, which seemed to waver and flicker
before her eyes ; if she touched it, if she
stretched out her hand, or found her voice,
would it not melt away ? Surely it would.
He was in South America. She unsteadily
moved out a hand, as one who gropes in the
dark. But that was no ghost's touch—no
phantom fingers which captured it, drew it,
her other hand, all of her, into a close embrace;
nor was it any unearthly voice which said :

'The aberration conquered at last, Sara. Your last letter came immediately after I had posted mine to you. I took it to mean that I might come.'

'You understood, Rudolf, at last?'

'At last, thickhead that I am, I thought I understood.'

'Ah!' said Sara, 'when I saw you come in, I thought you were of the same nature as a phantom—a dead man, who visited me last night, an evil spirit which I exorcised by the use of your name. I thought I saw your ghost, Rudolf.'

L'ENVOI.

SIX months later Jerome Wellfield was formally received into the Roman Catholic Church, in the large chapel at Brentwood; and six years later Nita's child was sent to the college of that name, there to begin his studies under the polished and accomplished supervision of the Fathers of the Society of Jesus.

Green wave the trees to this day over the river walk of Wellfield Abbey, and placidly that stream flows past the ruined cloisters, and under the wooded 'Nab.' The Abbey farms are as fat, and the Abbey lands as productive now, as they were in the days of its proudest fame. Once, years after these things had happened, a carriage, with a lady and a gentleman in it, drove through the village of Wellfield, over the bridge, away from John Leyburn's house. The persons in the carriage had been to pay a flying visit to John Leyburn's wife. As their carriage drove slowly up a steep hill just outside the village, they saw below them to the right the whole of the Abbey—the river, the avenue, even the ancient, hoary front of the house, and the lawn before it. It was a brilliant July evening, and they saw, slowly walking about that garden, three figures—that of a tall man, who held the hand of a slender, graceful-looking boy, whose face was turned towards his guide, and beside them, the figure of a priest, who appeared to be speaking earnestly, and who raised his hand now and then, as if to enforce his argument. The two travellers looked long at this group, and at the slender shadows they cast upon the dazzling green of the grass—as long as they could see it, until a bend in the road shut it all abruptly from their view : and then they looked, each into the other's face.

'What a life! What an ignominious slavery!' observed Falkenberg, with more than a tinge of contempt in his tone.

'If he finds peace in it, Rudolf?'

'*He!* And what about the poor child whom your friend was telling us about—what about his wife?

'I have often asked myself that question, and I can find nothing that gives me any answer to it—neither religion, nor irreligion, nor faith, nor unfaith. I told you long ago that Jerome Wellfield was as a dead man to me. And think of what he must feel himself dead to, before he could come to this. But he had no deliverer.'

They became silent until they drove into Burnham, from which town they were to

take the train to London, on their homeward
way. This was the last glimpse into
Jerome Wellfield's life which Sara ever
obtained or asked for.

THE END.